Max gave the family photo another look. "You seem like a close family."

A snort slipped out before Erica could stop it. At his surprised look she shook her head. "Looks can be deceiving. We're not close. It's been months since I've seen or talked to my parents. Things changed after Molly was taken."

He lifted a brow. "I'm sorry."

"Don't be. It is what it is. Maybe one day things will be different." *Only if you make an effort to change them,* said that little voice that was always right about such things. She cocked her head. "And maybe one day I'll tell you about it."

Max nodded and made his way to the door. "I'll see you in the morning. Sleep lightly and be careful," he said before he left.

She knew what he meant. He was worried about Peter.

Erica got that—she was worried, too.

I'll sleep with one eye open.

Not to mention with my bedroom door locked and my gun close by.

Books by Lynette Eason

Love Inspired Suspense

LYNETTE EASON

makes her home in South Carolina with her husband and two children. Lynette has taught in many areas of education over the past ten years and is very happy to make the transition from teaching school to teaching at writers' conferences. She is a member of RWA (Romance Writers of America), FHL (Faith, Hope, & Love) and ACFW (American Christian Fiction Writers). She is often found online, and loves to talk writing with anyone who will listen. You can find her at www.facebook.com/lynetteeasonauthor or www.lynetteeason.com.

HIDE AND SEEK
LYNETTE EASON

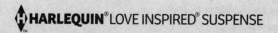
HARLEQUIN® LOVE INSPIRED® SUSPENSE

Recycling programs
for this product may
not exist in your area.

™ LOVE INSPIRED BOOKS

ISBN-13: 978-0-373-44548-6

HIDE AND SEEK

www.LoveInspiredBooks.com

Printed in U.S.A.

Look at the birds of the air; they do not sow or reap or store away in barns, and yet your heavenly Father feeds them. Are you not much more valuable than they?
—*Matthew 6:26*

To my wonderful Savior, who lets me write for Him. I also want to dedicate this book to my sweet niece, Willow Dorris, and my nephews, Jonah Dorris and Liam Dorris. Thanks for being such great kids and good friends as well as cousins to my kids. You guys rock!

Acknowledgments

Thanks to my family for all their support. This is my fifteenth Love Inspired Suspense book. I'm so thankful that you understand about deadlines and the desperation of pulling a plot and scenes from thin air—or your lives. (I suppose I should thank you for your forgiveness in this regard.) I love you all so much. I thank God for blessing me with you.

Thanks to Emily Rodmell, my Harlequin editor, for all her hard work on every single book I've written for Love Inspired. We made it to fifteen!

Thanks to Officer Jim Hall, who critiques and corrects all of my police procedural. If there's anything wrong in here, it's not his fault! Jim, you're awesome. So glad God dropped you into my life when you were living in North Carolina. God bless you!

Thank you to the ACFW Romantic Suspense loop and all of you who brainstormed this book and the next one with me. Thanks to Mary Lynn Mercer, Michelle Lim, Terri Weldon, Beth Ziarnik, Misty Kirby, Jeff Reynolds and Jessica Patch. You guys gave me some fabulous ideas, and even if I didn't use them all, you gave me some direction and inspiration. God bless each of you in your own personal writing journey.

ONE

Searching for a crack house had not been in Erica James's plans for the evening. However, Detective Katie Randall had uttered the one sentence that could send her into one of the worst neighborhoods in the city.

"We've found new evidence in Molly's disappearance."

Erica let the words ring through her mind as she drove, looking for the address of the crack house that had been raided two days ago.

New evidence. *New evidence.*

"It's been three years," Erica exclaimed. "What possibly could have come to light now?" she'd asked, hating the shakiness in her voice, the desperate hope that she knew was carved on her face.

Detective Katie Randall had shown her a photograph of a crime scene. Even now, Erica's fingers curled around the steering wheel as she remembered the little outfit clearly pictured amidst the trash and rubble.

The outfit three-year-old Molly had been wearing when she'd disappeared from the day-care field trip to the zoo. Erica touched the picture with a shaking finger.

"That's her hair bow."

"We got a fingerprint from it. A girl by the name of Lydia

Powell. Her prints are in the system for a shoplifting charge two years ago."

"So what does she say? Did you ask her about Molly?"

"We haven't been able to find her," Katie admitted.

"Then I will."

Now, two days later, on a cold Tuesday evening, Erica glanced at the sky. The sun would set in about ten minutes and she still hadn't found the address.

In this dark, dank part of town.

Drug deals on one corner, the selling of bodies and souls on the other. Her heart shuddered at the thought of her child being in the middle of all of this. And yet at the same time, her heart ached for the innocents trapped in this cycle of crime and abuse. For those who wanted out, but didn't know how to accomplish that. Or were too young to try.

Narrowed, suspicious eyes followed her progress down the trash-strewn street. The sun crept lower and her pulse picked up a notch.

As daylight disappeared so did the people on the street. One by one, everyone in a yard or on a porch made their way behind a closed, locked door.

She hadn't counted on it being dark by the time she got here. Then again, she hadn't counted on the place being so hard to find, either. Her GPS had led her down one street and up another until she was so twisted around she'd never find her way back out.

For the first time since Katie had told her the news, fear started to replace the hope she'd allowed herself to feel. She'd taken the information and run with it. Straight into one of the most dangerous parts of town.

What was she doing? Was she crazy?

After another hesitant second, she picked up the phone and dialed her brother, Brandon. Nerves on edge, she watched the street as she waited for him to answer. Finally, she heard, "Hello?"

"I think I've gone and done something stupid."

"Who, you? You're kidding." He didn't sound concerned—or surprised.

With good reason, she had to silently admit. She bit her lip. "No, Brandon, this time I'm serious."

That got his attention. "What is it? What's wrong?"

The mechanical voice from the GPS told her, "Turn left and your destination will be on the right." Erica rolled to a stop and looked to her left.

Brandon said, "Where are you?"

"Five sixty-seven Patton Street."

"Patton Street! Are you crazy?"

Now she heard the concern. "Yes, I think so. If I stay in my car and wait, will you meet me here?" Uneasy and on alert, she glanced around, felt unseen eyes watching her every movement. "Because while I'm not comfortable here, I'm not leaving yet, either."

She heard him muttering and thought she heard the words "crazy woman" in there somewhere. "I'm getting you home and then you're going into a safe occupation like accounting or—"

As Brandon continued his tirade, Erica chewed her bottom lip and tuned him out. Brandon worked with her at Finding the Lost, an organization dedicated to finding missing children she'd started after Molly disappeared. Erica, Brandon and Jordan—Brandon's best friend who'd needed a job and came highly recommended—worked together to find children who disappeared either through criminal activity such as kidnapping, or because they ran away.

Erica glanced in the rearview mirror and saw two rough-looking characters headed her way. Her stomach flipped. She whispered, "Oh, yeah, bad idea. Bad, bad idea." She had her self-defense training and her weapon, but—

"Bad idea is right. What made you decide to go there?" he demanded.

"New information about Molly's disappearance," she said with her eyes still on the rearview mirror.

Brandon paused then sighed, a small breath of understanding. "Ah."

Erica had to admit having a good working relationship with several police officers afforded her information she'd otherwise have trouble getting. Katie was her friend and Erica had proved herself trustworthy over the past couple of years. Which was why she now found herself in a possibly very bad situation.

A police cruiser rolled past on the street perpendicular to hers and the two figures behind her took off. She blew out a relieved breath, looked at her GPS one more time and turned left. And there it was.

"Give me about fifteen minutes," Brandon said. "Stay put."

The house she wanted loomed ahead on her right. She pulled to the curb two houses down and cut her engine, then her lights. The street lay empty, quiet as a tomb. She had a perfect view of the front of the house.

Night approached, sneaking in as though even it was reluctant to be found in this area of town.

"Erica? Did you hear me?"

"I heard you. I'll be waiting. A cop drove by and scared away the riffraff."

"If you're determined to stay, stay in the car with the doors locked. I mean it."

"Okay."

She had every intention of staying hunkered down in the front seat and waiting for Brandon to get there.

Until she caught a glimpse of a slim figure in a hoodie,

hunched over and slinking down the street toward the deserted house.

Erica's stomach twisted. She reached for the weapon she'd earned the right to carry in a concealed holster, but on second glance, the person didn't look to be a threat. Male or female? She couldn't tell.

Erica glanced at the clock, then back. The figure shot a look over a thin shoulder every so often. Finally, under one of the few working streetlights, Erica caught a glimpse of a pale face and scared eyes that flicked in every direction, watchful and jumpy. She looked to be about fifteen or sixteen and walked with quick jerky steps, shoulders bowed, arms crossed protectively across her stomach as though she wanted to make herself as small as possible.

Excitement spun inside Erica. This girl looked familiar. Could it be Lydia?

Did she need help? She kept looking over her shoulder.

Was someone behind her? Following her?

Erica watched for a few minutes until the girl disappeared around the side of the house. She put her hand on the door handle. If that was Lydia, she couldn't let her get away. She started to get out of the vehicle and stopped when she caught sight of another figure who had emerged from the shadows. He trailed the young girl, his steps quick and hurried.

Dread centered itself in the middle of her stomach. This didn't look good. Her fingers tightened on the handle, everything in her wanting to leap from the car. But she'd promised Brandon she'd wait.

When a shrill scream rent the night air, she could wait no longer. Erica threw open the door and raced toward the dark house.

Private investigator Max Powell shifted his eyes toward the older-model Ford Taurus parked on the street and leaned forward over the steering wheel as though that would give him a better view.

The car's open door and empty driver's seat set his nerves on edge. That didn't bode well. His gut tensed. Was his sister in that house? He'd gotten word from one of his street sources that she'd been here last night and would probably be back tonight. Max had rushed over to see if he could intercept her.

Max got out of his truck and peered inside the empty Ford. Relieved to see no evidence of foul play, he walked toward the house, his head swiveling in all directions, trying to discern whether there was a threat nearby or just someone who'd broken down and went looking for help.

Neither was a good option for the owner in this neighborhood.

Two feet away from the front porch steps, he stopped and checked the area one more time. The hair on the back of his neck stood at attention and adrenaline shot through his veins. He didn't have a good feeling about this—at all.

The brief thought that he should call one of his cop buddies flashed through his mind. But he wanted to find Lydia first, have a chance to talk to her before they found her.

He'd take his chances on going in alone.

He pulled his weapon and headed toward the front door.

Erica turned the corner around the back of the house and stopped. The door hung on one hinge, the darkness yawning beyond it now silent. In fact, it was so quiet, Erica wondered if it was possible she'd imagined the scream.

No. That had been real enough. Erica pictured the young girl she'd seen walking down the street. Her destination had been this house. Had that been her scream?

Her heart kicked into overdrive, pounding hard enough to make her gasp.

She swallowed hard and looked around. She couldn't just

stand here waiting for Brandon. Where was he? What if the girl needed help?

Nausea swirled in the pit of her stomach as she looked back at the house and thought about her precious baby being held in such a place.

A crack house.

One that kept its secrets hidden, maybe forever lost, her daughter's whereabouts never to be revealed. Had Molly cried for her, expecting her mama to come rushing in to save her?

The girl in the hoodie was someone's baby. And she might need help.

Tears clogged her throat even as she put one foot in front of the other to enter the black hole of a doorway. She hadn't been able to save Molly, but maybe she could help someone else's child.

She slipped just inside and moved to the left. The kitchen. The rancid smell of unwashed bodies, rotten food and...other odors she couldn't identify assaulted her.

Doing her best to ignore the offense to her nose, she listened. And heard nothing but her own ragged breathing. Erica moved farther inside. The moonlight sliced through the kitchen window to her left, casting shadows on the walls. Shadows that danced and mocked her. Should she call out?

Just as she opened her mouth, a creaking sound reached her ears. A thump sounded from down the hall, a scuffle. A muffled curse.

"Help!" a high scared voice called.

Erica dashed through the kitchen and into the hall. She tripped over the debris on the floor and managed to catch herself before she fell. Glass crunched beneath her feet, but she didn't stop. Light pierced the darkness behind her, illuminating the filth surrounding her.

"Hey! Who's in here?"

The deep male voice coming from behind her penetrated

Erica's fear even as she rounded the corner into the nearest bedroom only to come to a screeching halt.

A male in his midthirties had the girl by the throat with his left hand, a knife in his right. The girl's fingers clawed at his hand.

"Stop it!" Erica yelled. "Get away from her!"

Running footsteps sounded behind her. Erica moved and placed her back to the wall so she could see who entered the room, but she didn't want to take her eyes off the scene in front of her.

The attacker froze then shoved the crying young woman away from him and stepped toward Erica, knife raised, his eyes darting toward the door then back to her.

Adrenaline flowed, fear pulsed and she swallowed hard as she felt for the weapon in the holster just under her left arm.

In all the situations she'd found herself over the past three years, never once had she been forced to pull her gun.

It looked like tonight might be the night.

In the moonlight, she could make out the man's harsh features: glittering dark eyes and a scar that curved from the corner of his right eye to his jaw.

She shivered, notched her chin and demanded, "Leave her alone!"

"Stay outta this, lady, or you'll be sorry," he snarled.

"Drop the knife! Now!"

Erica whirled to see a man, weapon drawn and aimed at the young man in the torn jeans and black sweatshirt.

Blue lights flickered and flashed against the walls as backup arrived. The attacker licked his lips, shifted his feet.

"Drop it!" the man yelled again. The knife clattered to the floor. Erica nearly wilted with relief. "Up against the wall!" he shouted.

More footsteps sounded in the hallway as the man spoke

into his cell phone. Erica's head spun as she watched the young girl's terrified eyes snap to the man then to the window.

Before Erica could call out, the young teen ran to the window and climbed out.

"No! Lydia! Come back."

The man's shout hung on the empty air. Erica raced for the window, the breeze blowing back her blazer.

"Police! Hands in the air!"

She spun, shocked to see an officer's weapon trained on her.

TWO

Max spotted the concealed weapon under the woman's blazer and knew his pal, Officer Chris Jiles, had his gun on her. Her eyes, wide with shock, simply stared. Max brushed past her, careful to stay out of Chris's line of fire, and stopped at the window. Lydia was nowhere to be seen.

Max slapped a hand against the wall and spun as Chris said to the woman, "Put your hands on your head."

She finally blinked and said, "My name's Erica James. I...I have a concealed weapons permit."

"We'll get to that in a moment. Hands on your head." The woman complied and Chris stepped forward to remove her weapon from her holster. "Now show me some ID."

Max knew Chris had the situation under control, and he turned and dashed from the room. He raced down the hall and out the door. "Lydia!"

He spun to the left, then back to the right.

She was gone.

Heart heavy, he returned to the scene to find Chris's partner, Steve Shepherd, had the attacker on his knees. The man's hands were bound behind him and his cries of innocence fell on deaf ears.

Two other officers had gone after Lydia. Two more had cleared the rest of the house.

Max looked into the woman's face across from him. *Beautiful* pretty well summed her up—huge green eyes and curly red hair pulled back in a ponytail that accentuated high cheekbones. She had a fragile appearance that made Max want to offer his protection. Right after he questioned her and found out everything she might know about what just went down.

Chris ordered, "Let me see the permit."

"It's in my purse." She frowned. "Which is still in my car. Hopefully."

Chris looked at Max. "What are you doing here?"

"You have to ask?"

Chris scowled. "Right." Then he motioned for the woman to walk. Max followed them down the hall and out the front door. As they exited, Max heard, "Erica!"

Erica stopped and waved at the man, who looked like he was ready to start pounding the officers holding him back. "I'm all right, Brandon." Brandon gave her a fierce frown as she said, "Thanks for being willing to come to my rescue, but I didn't need you, after all."

His brows shot north. "What did you stumble into now?"

While she retrieved her license and showed it to Chris, she gave the man she'd called Brandon an abridged version of the events, which Max thought was still too long. She must have sensed his impatience because she finally said, "Go on back home, Brandon, I'll be all right now."

"I'm not leaving until I know you're home safe."

Max said, "I'll see to it she gets there."

Brandon rubbed his nose. "And you are?"

Max held out a hand. "I'm Max Powell. Former cop. Currently a private investigator."

Brandon shook Max's hand with a glare at Erica. "I'm Brandon Hayes, Erica's long-suffering older brother."

A sigh escaped her, and Max felt protective instincts surge to the surface once again. He couldn't help but wonder at his strange reactions to this woman. Maybe he was just stressed out and overly tired.

Erica stiffened, and Max saw her start to say something then stop. Finally she seemed to decide on her words. "Brandon, I'm fine. Go home. I'm sorry I called you out here on a false alarm."

The man wilted. "Aw, Erica…" He leaned over to give her a hug then shot a look at Max. "You're sure?" Max nodded.

"Go, Brandon. Jordan's probably wondering where you are," Erica said.

"Your boyfriend will be fine without me," Brandon said, giving Max a pointed look. The disappointment that shot through Max at the mention of Erica's boyfriend was just one more emotional surprise today.

"Knock it off, Bran. Just because you want him to be my boyfriend doesn't make it so. Now go home. I'll text you when I'm behind locked doors." She shot a look at Chris, who still held her license. "Hopefully they won't have bars on them."

Chris handed her wallet back to her. She spun away to stuff it into her purse as her brother got in his car.

He said, "I'll be checking on you."

"I'm sure you will."

Brandon pulled away just as the officers who had gone after Lydia returned—empty-handed. Anxiety twisted inside Max. Would he never be at the right place at the right time?

"Do you know the girl?" Erica asked.

He hedged. "Do you?"

"No."

Max watched as Steve led Lydia's attacker to the nearest cruiser and stuffed him in the back.

He felt her eyes on him. "But you do," she said.

"Why do you say that?"

She shot him a look full of exasperation. "Because you called her Lydia."

He nodded. "Yeah, I know her."

"I'm looking for a girl named Lydia, too."

Max stilled, tense. "Why's that?"

"Because she's a suspect in the kidnapping of my daughter three years ago."

The breath left his lungs. "You're Molly's mother?"

She paled. "You know who Molly is?"

"Of course I do. I've been following the story since I saw Lydia's face on the news."

"So who is she to you?"

Max blew out a deep breath and rubbed a hand over his head. "My sister."

Erica rolled with the shock wave. Of course. Lydia Powell, Max Powell. "Your sister?" she said. Anger swelled inside her. "Your sister had something to do with my daughter's kidnapping."

His eyes flashed. "She wasn't involved. She wouldn't do something like that. When I saw her face on the news, it floored me. To hear that she was wanted for questioning about kidnapping a three-year-old?" He shook his head. "She wouldn't. There's got to be some explanation."

Erica tucked her purse back behind her seat, thankful the car was exactly as she'd left it. She supposed having several police vehicles next to it had helped. "Well, I'd sure like to hear that explanation. And so would the cops."

His lips tightened and he narrowed his eyes. "What are you doing here?" he asked.

Erica lifted her chin, struggling a little to keep it together. "This is the house where my daughter was kept right after she was taken. When they did the raid last week, they found the clothes she was wearing when she disappeared. Along with the hair clip that had your sister's fingerprint on it. I couldn't believe that stuff was still here after three years. So

I came to see… I hoped…" Tears clogged her throat as her failure hit home.

Max swiped a hand across his eyes but not before she saw the brief flash of sorrow in them. He sighed. "Let's get this wrapped up here, and we'll talk. I want to know what you know about Lydia."

"And I want to know what you know." She slid into the driver's seat.

He spoke to the officers, and she focused on slowing her rapidly beating heart. Her emotions were on overload. She had accomplished nothing with her impulsive trip to the crack house.

No, that wasn't completely true. She'd found Lydia's brother. Maybe that was the first step in finding Lydia. She closed her eyes and leaned her head back against the headrest. *Oh, baby girl, where are you? Please Lord, help me find her.*

Sobs threatened once again as the helplessness overwhelmed her. With an effort, she focused on what she had to do next. The next step in the plan.

"I'll follow you home." She recognized Max's voice and opened her eyes.

She sighed. "It's all right. I can manage."

His jaw firmed. "It's late and you're in the toughest neighborhood in Spartanburg. Plus, I promised your brother I'd make sure you got home safe."

"I thought we were going to talk."

"We are." He tapped the hood of her car. "But you need some rest and I'm not through with my search for Lydia tonight." He paused and glanced at his watch. "Would you be able to meet for breakfast?"

Erica mentally went through her calendar. She had two appointments she could delegate. "What time?"

"Eight thirty?"

"Sure." She cranked her car.

Max pointed to the weapon that had been returned to her. "What made you feel the need to carry that?"

Erica felt a wry smile cross her lips. "A job that brings me into neighborhoods like this."

Curiosity lifted his brow. "What kind of job is that?"

"I find missing people. Children mostly." Sadness filled her. "I have a great track record, too. Mostly."

"Then why the sad eyes?"

She started, surprised he'd noticed. "It seems I can find everyone's child but my own."

He looked away for a brief moment, but not before she caught another flash of raw grief in his blue eyes. "Yeah. I know what you mean."

"Lydia?"

He nodded.

"She ran from you," she said softly. Even though she thought Lydia had something to do with Molly's disappearance, Max didn't. He obviously believed in his sister, and Erica's heart hurt for him. "I'm sorry."

He swallowed hard. "At least I know she's still alive. As of tonight anyway."

"Who was the guy attacking her?" Erica asked.

He frowned. "He's a punk who preys on young girls."

"A pimp?"

"That, and more."

She shuddered. "I'm sorry."

With another shake of his dark head, he straightened and gripped the door, ready to close it. "Which is why we need to talk. Tomorrow."

"Right." She let him shut the door and waited for him to get into his vehicle.

Relief that she'd survived this night swirled as her phone rang. She glanced at the caller ID. Jordan. She frowned. "Hey, is everything all right? Did Brandon get home okay?"

"Yeah. He told me what you'd been up to. I wanted to make sure *you* were okay."

"I'm fine." She was really tired of that phrase.

"Glad to hear it, but you're not home yet. I've been sitting on your front porch for the last few minutes and Mrs. Griffin is giving me the evil eye from her window across the street."

Mrs. Griffin. The street busybody who kept her nose in everyone's business, but was a sweet woman. "Why are you on my porch?"

Max flashed his lights to tell Erica he was ready, and she pulled away from the curb and made her way out of the neighborhood. She lived about ten minutes away, on the opposite side of town, and right now, all she wanted to do was get home, crawl into bed and sleep for a week.

But she couldn't. Not if Jordan was there.

Jordan was saying, "Because I care about you, Erica. Brandon does, too. He shouldn't have left you alone."

"I'm not alone." She grimaced. A sigh slipped out. "Look, go home." Those words were getting old, too.

Jordan paused. "All right. I'll just wait until you get here. Make sure you get inside safely."

"A P.I. is following me home. I'll be—" She refused to say it again. "All the drama is over." *Please don't add to it,* she finished silently.

"Okay." He didn't hang up. At this rate, he'd still be there when she pulled into the drive.

"So go."

"Right. I'll just be going."

Erica frowned. He sounded weird. "What's wrong with you?"

"Nothing. Nothing. I was just—"

"Just what?"

"Nothing. I'll talk to you tomorrow."

Erica hung up and glanced in the rearview mirror. Seeing

Max following behind her was comforting in an odd sort of way, even though she knew he had questions for her. That was fine—she had questions for him. And she would not notice his blue eyes again. Even though she had a feeling she could get lost in them, wondering what was going on behind them. Wondering what it would feel like to see them soften and sparkle for her. But she wouldn't do that. She couldn't. She wasn't interested in getting to know the brother of the girl who'd helped kidnap Molly. And she'd keep telling herself that as long as she had to in order to make herself believe it.

A few minutes later, she turned into her drive.

Jordan was gone and she breathed a sigh of relief. He'd been hovering like a mother hen lately—she couldn't figure out what was going on with him. And Brandon calling him her boyfriend just added to the confusion. Why would he say that? Jordan was a nice guy, but he was like a brother to her, and Brandon knew that.

Max pulled up against the curb and rolled the window down. Erica got out of her car and walked up to him. "Thanks for the escort."

"You want me to check out your house?"

"No thanks. No need."

"So. Tomorrow morning?"

"Yes." Her heart did a funny pitter-patter thing as his lips curved in a gentle smile. Shocked, she swallowed hard. She hadn't felt an attraction for a man in such a long time, she almost didn't realize what it was when it hit her. Ever since her husband had left her, she'd gone out of her way to avoid men. And now, in this crazy situation, she was finding herself attracted to a man she just met?

She shook it off and said, "We never picked a place."

"Where's your office?"

"On East Main Street in the same complex as the post office."

"How about the café?"

"I'll be there."

"You have your phone?"

Erica lifted a brow and pulled it out.

He gave her his number. "Call me if you need anything, or if something changes and you can't make it." She punched in the number and heard his phone ring. When she hung up, he nodded toward her house. "Now go inside while I'm watching. And lock the door."

"I always do." Irritated by his bossy manner, Erica turned and made her way into the house, twisting the dead bolt after shutting the door. The lamp on the end table next to her sofa gave off a soft light that reached into the foyer, casting friendly shadows on the wall beside her.

Much friendlier than the ones in the crack house.

Erica glanced out the window and watched Max drive away. Without his distracting presence, images from the night bombarded her and she shivered. "So close," she whispered to the empty room. So close to some answers, and once again they'd slipped away from her grasp.

Erica crossed to the mantel and picked up her favorite picture of Molly, the one taken the day before she disappeared. As always, the tears threatened, but she couldn't look away from Molly's bright smile, her unruly red hair pulled up into a ponytail and her green eyes glinting with good-humored mischief.

Well, the answers may have slipped away tonight, but at least she had a name to follow up on, thanks to Katie, and now she'd seen Lydia's face up close and personal. She would recognize her again when she saw her, even if she was still trying to hide beneath that hoodie.

Erica set Molly's sweet picture back on the mantel and turned to flip the lamp off.

Darkness covered her and for a moment she just stood

there, nearly drowning in her grief. It had been three years and still sometimes the pain of missing her child made her go weak.

Erica forced herself to head for her bedroom. She needed her rest. She would be no good for anyone if she let herself get to the point where she couldn't sleep again. Thankfully, she no longer needed medication most nights.

Tonight might not be one of those nights.

In her bedroom, she flipped on the closet light and let the warm light filter into the room. She wasn't in the mood for the strong overhead light tonight.

Just as she started for the bathroom to get ready for bed, she heard the distinctive click of the front door closing.

THREE

Max sat in his den staring at the file in front of him, wondering why he couldn't get Erica James off his mind. Her story touched him. Her fragile beauty drew him to her. But her accusations made him angry. The fact that she thought Lydia was involved with Molly's kidnapping made him more determined than ever to find his little sister and prove her innocent.

He ignored the little niggling of concern at the back of his mind that Erica might have a reason to be throwing her accusations out there.

Which was why he'd made a point of doing his homework on her.

Erica was twenty-eight years old, and had, by all appearances, been happily married until her daughter's kidnapping three years ago. Her husband had left and moved overseas about a year later.

Erica had pulled herself together and started her own business working as a skip tracer, learning how to use specialized equipment and unique skills to locate missing people—or in Erica's case, missing children. He remembered the sadness in her eyes, and what she'd said about being able to find other people's children and yet not Molly.

Thanks to his contacts at the police station, acquiring Molly's case notes hadn't been a problem. He flipped to the evidence section.

A witness had reported seeing a woman with red curly hair, large sunglasses and a long coat at the zoo that day. Another witness claims he saw a man following the preschool group. Too many reported seeing nothing unusual.

Curly red hair. Erica had curly red hair. But she had an airtight alibi. She'd been working another missing persons case and had even had a police officer with her.

And then there was the matter of that pain in her eyes. No, she hadn't had anything to do with her daughter's disappearance.

It had been a chilly day in November when Molly had gone missing. This month would be a tough one for Erica.

And now she was looking for Lydia. Max felt anger surface again. Twenty-one years old, his sister could pass for thirteen or thirty, depending on how close one looked. He supposed the drugs and sporadic eating could do that to a person. His heart ached for her. If only…

An idea hit him, and Max hauled himself out of the recliner and made his way into the kitchen to get his phone. He grabbed it only to frown as he saw an unfamiliar number listed, indicating he'd missed a call.

He dialed the number and listened to it ring.

When the phone went to Erica's voice mail, he hung up and felt the heat climbing into his face as he realized she'd called him earlier, when he'd given her his number. And here he was, calling her at nearly midnight. He shrugged. If she asked, he'd explain.

Then again, he couldn't help but wonder why she hadn't answered. Was she all right? Or had something happened?

He clenched his jaw.

He had no reason to think that anything had happened to her.

Just like he'd had no reason to think anything had happened to Tracy. His throat tightened at the thought of his fiancée, dead because he hadn't worried enough.

He'd ignored his instincts and she'd died.

Max grabbed his keys.

Erica's pulse pounded as she stood frozen, unsure what to do.

When the door had clicked, she'd raced into the bathroom and twisted the lock.

Leaving her cell phone on the end table in her bedroom.

She listened to it ring and put her hand on the knob. When it stopped, she bit her lip and looked around.

The only window in the bathroom was stained glass and didn't open. That cold hard knot in the pit of her stomach turned to granite as she realized what she'd done.

She'd trapped herself.

Desperately, she tried to control her ragged breaths so she could listen.

She pressed her ear against the door and heard nothing.

Except her phone ringing again.

Should she stay and assume whoever had entered her house would get what he was looking for and then leave?

Or should she try to slip into the bedroom and grab the phone?

Indecision warred with her fear. By the time she decided to stay put, the phone had stopped again.

How had her intruder come in the front door—the one she remembered locking? Mentally, she ran through a list of people who had a key to her house. Her brother, Brandon; her best friend Denise Tanner, who'd moved to New Mexico; her parents, although they'd only used the key one time in the past three years; another friend, Ginny Leigh, and…

Footsteps sounded outside the bathroom door. She gasped

and pulled back. He was in her bedroom. What would she do if he tried to get in the bathroom? Frantic, she cast her gaze around, looking for something she could use as a weapon.

A razor, a can of hair spray, the towel bar.

Then the steps receded. Faded. Stopped.

Was he gone?

Did she dare open the door? She waited. And listened.

Still nothing. Just the pounding of her heart.

The minutes ticked by.

Silence.

Her shaky fingers twisted the lock. She gripped the doorknob and turned it slowly, then pulled the door open a crack.

The door exploded inward and she cried out as the edge of it caught her on the chin. She fell to her knees as a tall figure reached down to grab her by the arm. "I knew you were in there."

"Let me go!" She twisted, kicking out and catching a shin.

Her captor grunted.

"Hey! Let her go!"

She froze once again. "Peter?" Disbelief made her dizzy. "What are you doing?" she cried. Peter approached her, his hands replacing her captor's on her arms.

Erica hit him in the chest to push him away from her, but he kept his grip on her upper arms. It didn't hurt, but she didn't like it.

"Hey, chill, sis. We just need some cash, okay?" His foul breath made her grimace.

"Let. Me. Go." She kept her voice low and did her best to rein in her fury and fear. Peter—her younger brother, the black sheep, the ne'er-do-well. Whatever one wanted to call him, he had also once been a suspect in Molly's disappearance but had been cleared when there'd been no evidence to support his involvement. He released her and she backed away from him until the back of her knees touched the bed. "Where did you get the key?"

"Let's get the cash and get out of here." Erica swiveled toward the man who'd grabbed her when she'd exited the bathroom. Menace dripped from his gaze.

Real fear clutched her. "Who's he?" she asked Peter.

Peter advanced. He stopped in front of her, but he didn't attempt to grab her again. His sullen, bloodshot eyes slid from hers, and she reached for the cell phone on the end table. "It's late, Peter, and I'm tired," she said, trying to sound normal. "I don't have any cash on me."

And she wouldn't give it to him if she did.

He was twenty-four and in spite of the drugs he pushed into his body, still looked young and innocent. He shot his buddy a black look. "I told you to wait outside."

"I got tired of waiting. You were looking in the wrong place." Drug-addled green eyes lingered on her and he licked his lips.

Peter stepped between her and the other intruder. "Back off, Polo. That's not what you're here for."

Polo leered. "Says you."

Peter stood tall and straightened his shoulders. "Yeah. I do. Now get out of here."

Erica blinked at Peter's defense of her. All of a sudden, she had a glimpse of the man he could have been.

Polo shrugged and backed down. "I'll be outside." He gave Erica one last look and she shuddered with distaste when he finally turned his back.

"Peter, get rid of that loser, then give me back my key." She paused for a moment, knowing she probably shouldn't say what she was about to say. "You can stay in the guest room tonight."

Peter lifted his hands and raked them through his hair. They trembled. He paced from one end of the room to the other, glancing at the door as though expecting Polo to return. "I need you to give me some cash. I'll give it to him, and he'll leave you alone."

What was he coming down from? His drug of choice was usually cocaine or heroin.

He shook his head. "I'm so tired." He sighed and rubbed his eyes. "Look, Erica, I'm sorry about all this."

She lifted a brow. "You're sorry?"

"Yeah. I'm—" He waved a hand. "I wish…"

"Wish what, Peter?"

Erica took his arm and tried to lead him from the room but he jerked away from her. "What are you doing?"

"Police! Anyone here?"

Peter froze like a deer caught in the headlights. "You called the cops?" he snarled.

"No! I didn't." She turned and yelled, "We're back here! Everything is fine."

Had they seen Polo?

Footsteps sounded on her hardwood and for the second time that night she faced the officers Max seemed to know personally, with their weapons drawn. She held her hands where they could see them. "Why are you here?" she asked.

"Everything all right?" The officer in front stepped forward, his narrowed eyes taking in the scene before him.

Erica nodded. "Yes. Fine."

The officers exchanged glances and the first one holstered his weapon. The second only lowered his.

"Who called you?" Erica asked.

"Your neighbor said she saw a suspicious man hanging around your front door. He was on his way over to see if you needed help when he heard you scream. Decided to call the cops instead." He motioned to the bruise on her chin. "Want to explain that?"

Erica looked at her brother as she reached up to touch her chin. "He surprised me and I got banged with the door."

Peter looked contrite. "I'm sorry. I didn't mean for you to get hurt."

Was he sorry? Or was he sorry he wasn't going to get what he came here for? She honestly didn't know what to think of him anymore. She just knew she wanted to help him, couldn't give up on him.

He was her brother, plain and simple.

The cop nodded, suspicion still written on his face. "What's he coming off?"

Pete glared at the officer and Erica sighed. "I have no idea, but I'll take care of him."

"You're not helping him by covering for him."

"I know." Weariness invaded her as she looked at her little brother. How had he become this stranger she didn't know anymore? Someone she didn't trust and was afraid of some of the time, like when he came into her apartment with a creep and tried to shake her down for cash? "He had someone with him. A guy named Polo."

Peter winced and the officer's eyes shot wide. "Polo Moretti?"

She grimaced. "I didn't get a last name." She looked at her brother. "Peter?"

"I just met the guy," Peter muttered. "I don't know his last name."

"Who is he?" Erica asked.

The two officers exchanged a glance. Then one said, "He's involved in all kinds of nasty stuff. You don't want to mess around with him."

Erica drew in a quick breath. "Peter, what are you involved in?"

"Erica?"

She frowned—she knew that voice. She shot a look at Peter to let him know the conversation wasn't over. "Max?"

Max stepped into the hall and greeted the officers by name. Then he looked at her. "What's going on? I kept calling but you didn't answer."

"So you drove over here?" Erica felt a thrill in the pit of her stomach that she couldn't explain but didn't want to think about.

"Yeah. It's not that far." Pain flashed in Max's gaze for a brief moment—long enough for her to wonder about it—until his gaze shifted to her brother, a question on his face.

Peter's eyelids drooped. He didn't seem so dangerous now. In fact he reminded her of the sleepy little brother she used to put to bed. Erica said, "Look, let me get Peter settled and we'll talk in the den."

Max and the other two officers left the room. "Go on in the bedroom. I'll take care of this," she said to Peter.

For once, he didn't argue with her, just shuffled his way down the hall with one last look toward the front door, probably wondering where his friend went.

If Peter stayed here, would that Polo guy come back looking for him?

She felt sick at the thought.

The guest room door shut with a decisive click. Erica stood staring at the door for a brief moment then shut her eyes as she fought the weariness that threatened to make her keel over. *Oh, Peter.* What was she going to do with him?

Voices from the den grabbed her attention. She'd worry about Peter later.

Erica made her way back into the den where she found Max sitting on her couch and the other officers standing in front of her fireplace looking at Molly's picture.

Max said, "This is Chris and Steve. You remember them from earlier tonight?"

Erica nodded, shook their hands and said, "Sorry for all the trouble. Peter's going through a rough patch and..." Her voice trailed off. What could she say? Peter's actions, the company he was keeping and his appearance spoke for themselves. She refused to make excuses for him anymore.

Chris nodded and said, "Just give us a holler if you need any more help with him." He paused. "But I'll caution you. Don't trust him."

She sighed. "I know."

After Chris and Steve asked her a few more questions and finally left, Max rose. "Guess I'd better be going, too." He glanced down the hall. "I'd feel better if he wasn't here."

So would she, but Erica wasn't going to tell him that. "Peter will sleep awhile and so will I. I'll talk to him in the morning, see if he's open to a plan—or rehab. Again."

Max nodded. "Okay." He rubbed his chin. "I talked to the detectives who handled Molly's case."

She lifted a brow. "Lee and Randall."

"Yes. Good detectives."

"Not good enough." The words left her lips before she could stop them.

He stuffed his hands into the front pockets of his jeans. "I can see why you would think that. But I work with them on a regular basis. And I'll tell you, not a week goes by that Katie—Detective Randall—doesn't review Molly's case. She keeps it fresh in her mind and is always ready for something to break. She's the one who recognized Molly's dress at the crime scene."

"Really? She didn't tell me that." Erica reached up to rub the rocklike muscles at the base of her neck. "Well, it's good to know they really do care," she said softly. She truly was touched to know that Katie reviewed Molly's case on a regular basis. Katie had become a friend during the nightmarish days and then months following Molly's disappearance. Erica had checked in with Katie regularly, but the woman had had nothing more to tell her.

Until the raid had unearthed Molly's dress and bow.

Erica watched Max walk over to her mantel and pick up the picture of Molly. "She looks like you."

Tears threatened, but Erica held them back. "Yes. She does."

He placed the picture back and looked at the others. "Your parents?"

"They live across town." Erica snagged the family portrait that had been taken at Christmas almost four years ago. "This is the brother you met tonight at the crack house—Brandon. He has a town house on East Main near our office. And this is Peter during one of his better times." She sighed. "He lives in our grandparents' old home on the west side of town. He doesn't have to pay rent so at least he has a place to sleep at night when he runs out of money." She reached out to trace a finger over Molly's image. "This is the last picture we had taken with all of us."

"And this one?" He pointed to the small silver and blue frame in the line.

Erica gave a sad smile. "That's Denise Tanner, my best friend. She and I were inseparable from third grade to graduation. We were even roommates before I got married. She lives in New Mexico now but we talk at least once a week."

Max placed a hand on her shoulder. "You've moved on. You haven't forgotten Molly or given up hope, but it hasn't broken you."

She could feel the warmth of Max's hand through her heavy sweater, and the sudden desire to lean into him and let him take a share of her burden nearly overwhelmed her. She resisted, but barely. "I didn't exactly have a choice and it hasn't been easy. But that's a story for another time." She really needed him to go or she was going to be a blubbering mess.

He gave the family photo another look. "You seem like a close family."

A snort slipped out before she could stop it. At his surprised look she shook her head. "Looks can be deceiving. We're not close. It's been months since I've seen or talked to my parents. Things changed after Molly was taken."

He lifted a brow. "I'm sorry."

"Don't be. It is what it is. Maybe one day things will be different." *Only if you make an effort to change them,* said that little voice that was always right about such things. She cocked her head. "And maybe one day I'll tell you about it."

Max nodded and made his way to the door. "I'll see you in the morning. Sleep lightly and be careful," he said before he left.

She knew what he meant. He was worried about Peter.

Erica got that—she was worried, too.

I'll sleep with one eye open.

Not to mention with my bedroom door locked and my gun close by.

FOUR

Max glanced at his watch for the third time in as many minutes. Was she coming? He sipped the cup of coffee he'd ordered and stared at the door, wondering if her brother or his "friend" had caused her any more trouble last night.

He frowned and shifted in his seat. How was he going to convince Erica that Lydia had nothing to do with Molly's kidnapping?

He finally concluded that he wasn't going to be able to convince her—not with words, anyway. He would have to show her who Lydia was, help her see his sister the way he saw her.

The mixture of smells in the café, such as cinnamon and coffee, tantalized him, making his stomach growl. The bagel and cream cheese in front of him was going to be too much temptation to resist if he had to wait on her much longer.

Max pulled out his phone, ready to punch in Erica's number when the door finally opened and she stepped inside, bundled against the frigid November wind.

She spotted him and smiled.

He waved her over.

Erica settled into the seat across from him and he said, "Any trouble last night?"

She shook her head. "He was gone when I got up this

morning. I heard him leave around five o'clock." And she hadn't asked him to stay.

"Does he show up like that very often?"

"Every once in a while. That was the first time in about three months."

And Peter had never brought anyone with him before—the appearance of Polo Moretti was new. Erica wasn't sure what to make of that yet.

"You want some coffee?"

"Yes, I'll be right back."

Max sat back to study her as she headed to the counter to order. He decided he could look at her for a long while without growing bored. Very pretty, with auburn curls and green eyes. She was also tall. He put her at around five feet eight inches or so.

Within minutes, she had her coffee and a pastry, and she settled back into her seat with a sigh. "It was a long night, but we survived."

"Indeed." He rested his elbows on the table and clasped his fingers together in front of him. "Do you mind if I say a blessing?"

Erica set her coffee cup down. "Of course not."

Max bowed his head and thanked God for the food and for His guidance in finding Lydia and Molly. Short but effective. He saw Erica blink away tears and take a deep breath.

His heart ached for her loss. He couldn't even imagine what it must be like to have someone steal your child. Not knowing where his sister was nearly ate him alive, but if it was his child…

Erica took a bite of her pastry, which dripped with chocolate sauce, and said, "Do you mind telling me about your sister?"

Max sighed and said, "It's not a pretty story." Of course, in telling her about Lydia, he would also be opening himself up and revealing information he didn't share with just any-one. She must have seen this on his face because she reached across the table and placed her hand over his.

"Please," she said.

Max felt his stomach twist at her touch.

She thinks Lydia had something to do with her daughter's kidnapping, he reminded himself.

He drew his hand away and snagged his coffee cup. Her face flushed and she clasped her fingers in her lap. Guilt hit him. He hadn't meant to make her feel awkward.

"Look, Lydia's not perfect by any stretch of the imagina-tion. And I know she's a suspect, but I really don't think she would have anything to do with kidnapping."

Erica gave a small shrug and her lips tightened. "I don't know your sister, of course. I only know that her fingerprint was found on the bow Molly was wearing when she disap-peared. That makes me want to find her and talk to her. And if she didn't have anything to do with it, why is she running?"

He had to admit that running didn't look good, but that was typical Lydia. She ran from problems instead of facing them whether she was guilty of causing them or just in the wrong place at the wrong time. "I want to find her, too, give her a chance to explain."

Erica took a sip of her coffee and studied him. She finally asked, "Can we work together?"

He paused. Work with her? Maybe. Keep an eye on her? Definitely. "I think we can. But you have to understand I'm looking to prove she didn't have anything to do with the kid-napping."

Erica nodded. "I'm not looking to prove her guilty of anything—I'll leave that to the cops. I just want to talk to her, find out what she knows. Ask her why her fingerprint was on my daughter's bow."

He could live with that. For now. Plus, keeping her close

and under his watchful eye would be better than having her go off on her own and finding Lydia before he could.

"All right," Max said, "I'll tell you Lydia's story."

Erica waited while Max gathered his thoughts. Her nerves danced and her heart pounded. She wasn't sure if it was due to the man seated across from her or what he was about to say. She reluctantly admitted it was probably a combination of both.

Max had dark good looks, and his no-nonsense attitude matched her own. She liked that he was willing to work with her even though he knew she thought it was very possible Lydia had something to do with Molly's kidnapping.

She liked him. Period. And for the first time in a long time, she wanted to see if she would still like him the more she got to know about him.

But for now, Lydia was her priority. Erica couldn't afford to have romantic feelings, not when there was a new lead in Molly's case.

"The short version," Max said, "is that Lydia and I grew up in the neighborhood you found yourself in last night."

Erica hadn't expected that one. "Oh wow."

"Yes. It was a bad situation. Our parents were also products of that neighborhood. I'm eight years older than Lydia so by the time she came along, I was already a seasoned pro at staying out of the way of the fights and the drug dealers." He shrugged. "I felt like I had to protect her, but for an eight-year-old that was a lot."

"No eight-year-old should face a responsibility like that," she whispered, appalled and yet amazed he'd survived to become the man he was today. "Why are you different? How did you get out?"

He gave her a rueful smile. "Foster homes. One of them anyway. I learned that the world was not just pain and drugs and abuse. I learned about love and God, and that if I wanted to climb out of the hole that was my life, I could do it as long as I wasn't afraid of hard work." He rubbed his chin. "You want to hear something silly?"

"Sure." Her fingers curled into her palms as she fought the urge to offer comfort.

"I watched a lot of movies growing up, and I saw these families portrayed as loving, kind to one another. Not perfect, but definitely not like my family." He gripped his knife and looked at it, then laughed—a sad, derisive sound. "I used to picture my family sitting around me at Thanksgiving or Christmas while I carved the turkey."

"And you wanted a family like that?"

"Yeah." He flushed and shook his head. "I don't know why I told you that."

"It's okay," she said softly. This time she didn't fight her feelings. Erica reached over and squeezed his hand. "I know exactly what you mean."

He shook his head. "So anyway, I guess you see that we didn't have a great childhood."

"But you rose above it. So many people don't. What happened with Lydia?"

Pain flashed in his eyes. "I lost touch with her for a while. When I turned eighteen, she was ten and a ward of the state. I didn't find her again until she was sixteen. She's the reason I quit the force and turned to private investigating. I could spend more hours on tracking her down as a P.I. than I could as a cop. When I finally found her, I asked her to come live with me, but she was pretty happy with her foster mother, a woman named Bea Harrison. So I didn't push the issue. The next time I went to visit her, though, she was gone." His mouth tightened at the memory and his eyes flashed.

"Did you find her again?" She knew Lydia was alive as of last night, but she still tensed as she waited for his answer.

He took a bite of his bagel and nodded. "Yes. Turns out our

mother had gone through some kind of program and completed it successfully. And the court gave Lydia back to her."

Erica gaped. "What?"

"I couldn't believe it, either. I was furious. I went to the house and found Lydia high and my mother passed out on the couch. Alcohol and drugs were everywhere." He swallowed hard. "I called DSS and the cops and waited for them to get there. They took her back into the system, and Lydia has been mad at me ever since."

Erica swallowed hard. This was the girl Molly had possibly been with? What had her child experienced while with her? Erica shut off that line of thought. She just couldn't go there.

Max was saying, "I finally got custody of her about two months before she turned eighteen, but she refused to stay with me. The court sent her back to Bea, and Lydia agreed to that arrangement as long as I wouldn't come around. The only time she talks to me now is to beg money for a hit." He paused. "I had hoped things were turning around when she agreed to let me take her out on her eighteenth birthday. Things were definitely looking better between us, but about a month later, she was back to her distant, I-hate-Max self."

Her heart ached for him. "I'm so sorry."

Max ran a hand down his face. "She was stabbed around that time and ended up in the hospital. I never found out what the circumstances were, but she almost died. I sat with her day and night, hoping to show her how much I loved her, but once she was released, she disappeared again. Over the last three years, we've had minimal contact." He grimaced at Erica. "There—you have the whole ugly story. You sure you don't want to run screaming in the other direction?"

"No, your story doesn't scare me. It makes me hurt for you and Lydia, but it doesn't scare me."

She thought she saw relief in his eyes before he glanced out the window.

"I hate to point this out, Max, but Lydia's lifestyle makes it more likely that she would be involved in something like Molly's kidnapping than not."

His jaw hardened and she could tell he didn't like her statement. "You don't know her. I do."

"Do you really? You said yourself you two have been estranged, and she will hardly even talk to you. How can you claim to know her?"

Max's nostrils flared. "You'll just have to trust me on this."

Erica bit her lip. "I'm not deliberately pushing you, but surely you can understand where I'm coming from. Her fingerprint was found on the bow."

He nodded. "I get that. But I'm sure there's an explanation for it. Which is why I want to find her. To help her. Because the police aren't going to care about helping her." He brought his intense gaze back to Erica. "I'd really like to find her first."

I'm sure you do, Max. And I plan to be there when it happens.

"You said you'd gotten custody of Lydia before she turned eighteen. Does she still have a room at your house?"

He lifted a brow. "Yes."

"Do you mind if I take a look at it?"

"She doesn't stay there." He looked away. "I keep it for her, hoping one day she'll show up and want to work things out."

"You didn't do anything wrong."

"Maybe not, but maybe I could have handled it differently. Instead of calling DSS, I could have just taken her out of there and…" He shrugged.

"And maybe not. If there's anything I've learned over the past three years, it's that we can't avoid making mistakes, and when we do, we should learn from them. Unfortunately, you can't rewrite the past."

"I know." He offered her a sad smile.

"So what happened to your parents?"

"My dad was killed in a car accident about seven years ago. After I called the cops on her, my mom went back to jail for possession. When she got out, she went right back to drugs and died from an overdose."

Erica gasped. "How awful, Max. I'm so sorry." She couldn't seem to find any other words. No child should have to live the way he and Lydia had, scrambling and scraping to survive.

He sighed. "I couldn't help her, but I'm going to do my best to help Lydia."

"I understand. That's how I feel about Peter." She paused. "I still want to see Lydia's room. Do you mind?"

He shook his head. "She's only stayed there a handful of times. Mostly when Bea caught her doing something wrong. Since I actually had custody, it wasn't something her social worker worried about. And after she turned eighteen she was out of the system anyway."

If Lydia had been in that room for even one minute, Erica wanted to see it. "Do you mind if I ride with you, or do you want to take me to my car?"

"I don't mind driving. Come on."

Erica's mind clicked with renewed hope. Seeing Lydia's room was a great start. Something the cops hadn't had access to three years ago—simply because they hadn't known about it. Praying the room would lead somewhere, she got into the car.

On the drive to his house, Erica checked in with her office. Rachel Armstrong, Erica's cousin, answered the phone. "Hey, Rachel, anything I need to know about?"

"No, it's kind of slow right now," Rachel replied. "You've got two calls to return, though—the parent of a runaway and someone who wants a status update."

"Okay." Erica gave instructions for the update and then

said, "Give the parent of the runaway to Jordan. I'm working on this lead we've got on Molly."

"A lead on Molly? Really?"

"Yes." The hope mingled with sadness in Rachel's voice tugged at her. Rachel had loved Molly like her own. "I'll be praying it pans out."

Rachel, along with other family members, had given up hoping that Molly would ever be found. Erica didn't hold it against any of them, but she refused to join ranks. She hoped, she believed, she prayed and she searched. And she'd never give up. Ever.

As a result of her obsession with finding Molly, she'd pushed a lot of her family away, including her own parents. With a start, she saw the parallels between her life and Denise's. When Denise's husband had left her, she'd also pushed away her family and friends and focused on her job. Denise allowed her work to consume her. Erica had allowed finding Molly to do the same.

Acting on impulse, Erica said, "What are you doing tomorrow night, Rachel? Want me to bring over some Chinese and we'll play Scrabble until we can't think straight?"

"Seriously?" The stunned tone in Rachel's voice caused Erica to wince.

"We haven't done that in forever. It'll be like old times."

"Oh, I'd love to, Erica. That sounds like a ton of fun, but I already have plans tomorrow. What about another time?"

"Sure, you let me know when," Erica said. "But soon, okay? I need some girl time."

"You bet."

Erica hung up and chewed her bottom lip. Was she too late to reconnect with her cousin? She hoped not. She hoped Rachel was simply busy and not avoiding her. Vowing to do better at reaching out to the people in her life, she stared out the window.

Cutting into her thoughts, Max asked, "How many people do you have working for you?"

"We're a crew of four right now." Erica tucked the phone in her jacket pocket. "There's me and Brandon, who was a detective on the police force but gave it up to help me put this business together. And then Brandon's best friend Jordan joined us. He was with the FBI, but he quit." She shot him a sidelong glance. "I still don't know the whole story. Maybe one day he'll feel like he can share it."

"You've got a lot of skills and resources at your disposal. What about Rachel?"

"She's my cousin. She's also the administrator—she answers the phones and does whatever office work needs doing. She and I used to be much closer than we are now." She sighed. "It's time to do something about that." The last sentence was more for her than for him.

"Sounds like quite a team."

"I don't mind bragging a little—it really is an amazing—"

Max slammed his foot on the brakes and Erica's seat belt locked hard as she rocked forward, crushing it against her chest. Tires squealed, horns blared—and Erica screamed as a green car came straight at her.

Max turned the wheel a split second before the other vehicle hit, managing to avoid the worst of the collision. Like fingernails on a chalkboard, the green car scraped down the passenger side and Erica felt herself thrown against the seat belt once again.

Max brought his truck to a shuddering stop.

"What happened?" Erica gasped.

"That guy ran a red light," he said. He reached out and grasped her arm. "Are you all right?"

"I think so."

The green car quickly backed up and spun into a three-point turn. "He's leaving," Erica warned.

Max grabbed his phone. "I have a hit-and-run to report. License plate is NRV444." He looked at her. "Are you sure you're all right?"

Erica took a moment to gather her wits and make sure she was still in one piece. "Yes. Yes, I'm fine. Are you?"

He nodded. "It looks like the only real damage is to the car, thank goodness."

A knock on her window made her jump. She tried to roll the window down but she couldn't. Next she tugged on the door handle. "I can't open the door, Max. It's stuck."

He opened his door and she crawled across the seat, letting him help her out onto the asphalt. Questions from the bystanders and witnesses started instantly. The police arrived, and Erica felt her head begin to pound.

There was something about that green car....

An officer approached her. "Hey, you look really pale. Do you need to sit down? Do you need an ambulance?"

She felt Max take her arm and lead her away from the cop to the curb, where he helped her sit. "Take a minute and get your breath."

She looked up at him. "I think I know who hit us."

"You saw the driver?" Max asked.

"No. But I saw the car."

His eyes narrowed. "And you recognized it?"

"Maybe."

"Who does it belong to?"

"Well, I didn't get a good look, but I'm pretty sure it was my brother Peter's."

FIVE

Erica waited while Max shared all the information he could with the officers and they promised to get a BOLO—a Be On the Lookout—on the vehicle and find Peter for questioning. He looked at Erica, who had risen from the curb to pace. "Do you want me to take you home?"

"I think we need to find Peter."

"The cops are going to be looking for him."

"I know. Which is why I want to find him first."

"Where do you think he is?"

She sighed. "He has a job doing construction. When he's sober, he's working but it's a different job every week. But if that was him in the car…"

"You want to try his house first?"

"Okay."

"Then let me tell the officers we're leaving and we'll head over to see if Peter's at home. I'm pretty sure my truck is drivable."

She nodded. "I'll see if I can reach him on his phone. Depends on if he has any minutes or not."

While she tried Peter, Max let the officers know they were leaving and to contact him if they needed anything else.

As they drove, Erica tried Peter again. "He's not answering his phone. Who knows where he is?" She chewed her bottom lip.

"We'll find him." He glanced at her. "You're going to be sore. You really flew into that seat belt."

"I'll be all right. I'll take something if I need to."

They rode in silence for the first few minutes then he asked, "So how do you fit in?"

She blinked at the out-of-the-blue question. "What do you mean?"

"With your company. You told me all about everyone who works there. What about you?"

Erica sorted through what to tell him, then decided to just lay it out there. "After Molly disappeared, I spent all my money trying to find her. At least all the money I could get my hands on. My husband…" She gave a heavy sigh. "My marriage fell apart. We tried counseling, but by that time…" She waved a hand. "Anyway, I just couldn't give up on finding Molly. I had to be doing something, not just waiting for the phone to ring. So I picked the career that would allow me to do that. I became a skip tracer and I specialize in finding missing children."

"While you keep searching for Molly."

"Yes." She pointed. "Turn here."

Max turned into Peter's subdivision and followed her directions until she motioned to the one-story house on the corner. "It's nice."

Her lips quirked into a wry smile at his surprise. Junkies didn't usually have nice places to sleep. "I pay for someone to do the yard each week. I don't want the neighbors complaining." She frowned. "I don't recognize the car at the curb."

Max had noticed the black Mustang, too.

"He may have company." She hesitated. "Inside is pretty bad most of the time. Every once in a while I'll come over to check on him and clean up some. It's been a week since I've been here so no guarantees about what it looks like in there."

He nodded. "I've seen worse, I'm sure."

She knocked on the door and waited. Then knocked again.

Max was ready to concede Peter wasn't home when the lock clicked. The door swung open and Peter stood there blinking in the sunlight, unshaven and offensive to Max's nose.

Erica acted as though she didn't notice. "May we come in?"

"Why?"

Impatience tightened her features. "Because we need to talk to you before the cops get here."

That seemed to wake him up a bit. "Cops? Why'd you call them? I thought all that was straightened out last night. I just needed some cash."

"For a hit." Erica glared at him. "Looks like you found some."

Pain flashed in his eyes for a brief moment then a silly smile crossed his dry, cracked lips. "Yeah. I did. Polo hooked me up. He's got this friend named Sandy—"

Erica pushed her way inside. Peter stopped his explanation and didn't protest, so Max kept his mouth shut and followed.

And wished he'd volunteered to wait outside.

Body odor and spoiled food assaulted his nose. Erica gagged and walked into the kitchen to the right. She shook her head and came back into the tiny foyer. "I'm not going to lecture."

"Good. 'Cuz I'm not going to listen."

Polo stumbled from the rear of the house. "Who is it?"

Peter sighed and rubbed his bleary eyes. "My sister and her friend. Let me take care of this."

Polo eyed Erica. Then his gaze slid to Max. "She belong to you?"

"Yeah," Max said before Erica could answer. He stared Polo down until the man gave a short nod.

"Bummer." He looked at Peter. "Get 'em outta here. We got business."

"Cops are on the way. You better vanish. Business can wait."

With a glare at Erica and Max, Polo slipped out of the house. Within seconds, they heard the roar of the motor and the squeal of tires as he pulled away from the curb. Erica looked at Peter. "Were you at the corner of Henry and East Main earlier today? Like about an hour and a half ago?"

Peter squinted. "No, man. I was asleep. I haven't left the house since I got home from Sandy's."

Knowing junkies sometimes got their facts skewed, Max asked, "What time was that?"

A shrug. "I don't remember. Probably around eight o'clock this morning."

"And you didn't leave again?"

"I said no."

"When did your friend show up?"

"About ten minutes before you did. He woke me up."

"Where's your car?"

He gave her a puzzled look. "In the garage where I always keep it when I'm not using it. What's with the third degree?"

Max said, "Your car sideswiped us this morning."

"What?" He laughed. "Not possible." Peter shook his head and walked through the kitchen. He opened a door that probably led to the garage.

And gaped.

He spun. "It's not there." He paced to the sink and back to the door again. "Where's my car?"

"That's what we want to know," said Max's cop buddy from the front door where he stood next to his partner. "Peter Hayes?"

Peter held his hands up. "I wasn't driving. I swear."

"Can anyone give you an alibi?"

He swallowed hard. "I was asleep. I didn't even know my car was missing."

Chris and Steve exchanged a glance, then looked at Max. "What are you doing here?"

"The same thing you are."

"We got the hit-and-run you called in."

Max gestured to Erica. "She recognized the car."

"But he wasn't driving it?"

Erica shook her head. "I don't think so."

"I wasn't!" Peter said. "I want to report a stolen car." He ran a hand through his greasy hair. "I can't believe someone stole my car."

Max snorted as Peter muttered a few more dire threats on the head of the person responsible for the missing vehicle. He looked at Chris. "This the first time this has happened?"

"Yeah. I checked to see if he was a repeat, but he's not." Max was surprised. A missing car was a common call from drug addicts. They often loaned their vehicle to their addict friends and when the friend didn't bring it back, they filed a stolen vehicle report.

Erica managed to calm her brother down enough to sit on the sagging couch.

Chris pulled out his notebook and said, "Tell me, in detail, where you were this morning and who would have taken your car?"

"I don't know! That's why you're here, right? To find out?"

The man truly looked distressed. Max began to wonder if he wasn't telling the truth.

Chris continued. "Who has the keys?"

"The keys were probably in it," Peter mumbled.

"Uh-huh. And what crackhead did you loan it to?"

"I didn't loan it to anyone." Peter sighed and ran a dirty

hand through his greasy hair. Max saw Erica wince and turn her face from the man's odor.

"All right, give me the description of the vehicle, the tag number, make and model, color and all that."

As Peter provided the information, Erica massaged her sore shoulder, and Max said, "Come on. We can't do anything else here. Let's get you some Ibuprofen then we can head to my house and I'll show you Lydia's room."

They left Peter to fill out his stolen car report and to re-tell his story to the officers. Max wondered if they'd believe him, but as of right now, they didn't have any proof to refute the story. Max knew Chris and Steve would continue to investigate the accident. He just hoped for Erica's sake that her brother wasn't lying.

Erica looked at the modest brick two-story from Max's driveway. "Very nice."

"I bought this house about four years ago." Pride echoed in his words. "I'd never owned anything in my life. I lived mostly in apartments while trying to go to school and just keep my head above water financially, but when I decided to get custody of Lydia, I wanted someplace special to bring her."

Together they walked toward his front door. Erica couldn't help a glance over her shoulder, wondering at her feeling of being watched. She forced herself to brush it aside. Once inside the house, her uneasiness disappeared and she gasped in delight. "It's beautiful. Did you decorate this yourself?"

A flush crept up into Max's cheeks. "Well, I did the woodwork, the molding and the painting. A friend of mine helped me out with the decorating aspect."

A friend? Erica couldn't help wondering if that friend was more than just a "friend." A little dart of jealousy shot through her and she stood still, shocked by the feeling. Not wanting to dwell on it, she turned back to admiring his home. Shiny hardwood floors made her pause. "Should I take off my shoes?"

He laughed. "No. You're fine."

A simple, classy chandelier hung overhead. Stainless steel appliances and granite graced the kitchen to the right. "It's truly lovely."

He motioned toward the steps. "Lydia's room is upstairs."

Erica followed him up the steps, her fingers trailing over the banister. At the top, he turned left and entered the first room on the right. Erica stepped inside and was once again impressed. "I can't believe she didn't want to stay here. It's charming, but simple enough she could put her own stamp on it if she wanted to."

Max gave her a warm yet sad smile. "Yeah, well, I'm still not her favorite person so—" He shrugged, and she could tell his heart was heavy.

She laid a hand on his arm. "Maybe she'll come around soon."

"Maybe."

Even though she felt sorry for Max and the angst his sister was putting him through, she still couldn't get past the fact that the evidence pointed to Lydia's guilt. She removed her hand.

"What if she's staying away because she's guilty and she's afraid you'll turn her in to the cops?"

He sighed and dropped his head. "It's more likely that she's staying away because she believes that I think she's guilty. That's one of the reasons I have to find her. I have to convince her that I believe in her."

"Do you have to convince her? Or yourself?"

Max stared at her. "You've already got her tried and convicted."

"And you've bypassed the evidence and are letting your emotions get in the way."

Max held up a hand. "We've agreed to disagree. Can we please not argue about it?"

Erica sighed and looked at the closet. "May I?"

"Sure."

She opened the door and saw a few outfits and several shoe boxes lined up on the shelf. She went through them, hoping to find anything that might lead her to Lydia. Disappointment spiked when she only found shoes that would appeal to a young woman. "Did you buy this stuff for her?"

"Yes."

"You've got good taste."

He gave a short laugh and pulled open the top drawer of the dresser. "I've searched her room each time she's stayed and never found anything." He rummaged through the next drawer. "I think she figured I'd search and just didn't bother bringing anything here."

Erica planted her hands on her hips. "You could have told me that."

His sad smile speared her. "You needed to see for yourself."

He was right. She gave a slight nod of acknowledgment, and they finished the search together in silence.

They came up empty.

Erica ran a weary hand over her face. "Well, it was worth a try. Thanks for letting me look." She thought for a moment then said, "Do you have time to go to Bea Harrison's house?"

He glanced at his watch. "I can call her and see if she's home."

"That would be great."

As Max called, Erica stepped outside in the chilly afternoon air.

From the corner of her eye, Erica noticed a green car rolling down the street. "Max, I think that's my brother's—"

A gunshot cracked and wood from the porch roof rained down on them.

SIX

Erica screamed and ducked. Max grabbed her against him, shielding her with his body as he fell back inside his house and kicked the door shut. "Get behind the sofa and crouch down."

He peered out the window. The vehicle sat in the middle of the street in front of his house. His blood pounded through his veins as he saw the barrel of a rifle appear in the open passenger window.

He ducked back down. Another burst of gunfire erupted. Windows shattered as he hunkered beside the front door. Max winced as flying glass grazed his face. Heart thudding, he waited.

He could hear Erica on the phone with a 911 operator, giving a status report in a shaky voice.

Tires squealed on the street out front and Max peered through the broken window. The green car shot down the street and the sudden quiet echoed in his ears.

People peered from behind pulled curtains. Doors opened and curious neighbors with stunned expressions stepped out onto their porches once they realized the threat was gone.

"Erica," Max called, "are you all right?" He rushed into the den to find her still on the floor behind the couch, phone pressed to her ear.

Pale and shaken, she looked up and nodded. "Are you?"

"Yeah."

"The cops are on the way."

He helped her up and felt her pulse jumping under his fingers. "That was pretty close."

She swallowed hard. "Too close." She searched his face. "So is someone after me? Or you?"

He lifted a brow and pursed his lips. "That's a really good question."

"You have some enemies you need to tell me about?"

He smirked. "The list is endless."

"I've made a few people mad in my line of work, too."

He shook his head. "I really can't think of a way to narrow the list, but I'll call Chris and see if he'll look into it. I can think of four or five characters I've arrested who've made threats to get even. We'll see what they're doing now."

"And I'll get Jordan or Brandon to look into the same thing on my end." She chewed her lip. "Although I have to say I really think this is somehow related to this search for your sister."

He wanted to protest, but he didn't have any proof that she was wrong, so he didn't argue. And he couldn't say the thought hadn't crossed his mind.

Sirens sounded as law enforcement descended. Chris bolted from his cruiser as Max stepped outside. Chris shook his head. "I recognized your address over the radio. You okay?"

"Yeah. Just a drive-by with lousy aim, fortunately."

Chris eyed him with a frown. "Man, I've seen you more in the past twenty-four hours than I ever did when we actually worked in the same precinct. What have you got going on? Someone tries to take you out in a hit-and-run this morning, then this?"

"I know." Max knew the two incidents were related. There

was no doubt it was the same car, thanks to the scrape alongside the passenger-side door. "I'm looking for Lydia. That's the only thing I can think of."

"Someone doesn't want you to find her?"

"Lydia doesn't want me to find her, but I don't think she'd shoot at me."

"And I don't believe Peter would try to run us off the road," Erica said.

Max looked doubtful and asked Chris, "Do we have a location on Peter while this shooting was going on?"

Chris shook his head. "We left soon after you did. We're not ruling him out. He's still a suspect and it's very possible he's hiding the car, but right now there's no evidence. Although the plate I got this morning was definitely registered to Peter. We're going to keep looking into this and keep an eye on him."

"Great." He glanced at Erica. "Because the car that was involved in the drive-by was the same one from this morning."

"What? Peter's?"

"Yeah." Max drew in a deep breath. "Looks like we need to ask him some more questions."

Max watched the officers question neighbors and put up the crime scene tape. The crime scene unit started looking for the bullets.

An hour later when they'd talked to everyone they could find that might have seen something, the officers left.

Erica gave him a weary smile and glanced at her watch. "I need to get going."

"I'll drive you. Where to?"

"I volunteer at the community church on Main Street serving meals to the homeless."

Max gave her a hard look. "The homeless? Why would you want to be around people like that?"

She blinked. "People like that?"

"A lot of them are criminals. They'll take advantage of you the moment your back is turned. Or kill you."

Shock made her blanch, then her face turned red. "Really? That's what you think about the homeless? How sad." She shot him a look full of anger mixed with pity. "Forget the ride. I'll get someone else to drive me."

Max watched her stomp off and winced. He'd obviously offended her, but she was just such an innocent when it came to watching out for herself. Someone had to do it. Right?

Possibly, but he could have phrased his concerns better. Been less blunt. Just because his experience with the homeless hadn't been ideal didn't mean he could push his feelings on Erica.

He'd have to apologize and explain his strong reaction. She still had her stiff back toward him. That is, he'd explain if she gave him a chance.

Erica sat at her desk and stared out the window. Twice today her life had been in danger. And twice today, she'd been involved in giving statements to the police.

Of course Max could say the same. She thought about his negative reaction to her charity work and tightened her jaw. She had to forget about that for now and focus.

She wanted to find Lydia.

Max had called to say that Bea Harrison hadn't answered her phone but that he'd keep trying, and let Erica know when he reached her. His words had been stilted, but not rude. She'd kept her attitude chilly but polite. She supposed she should apologize.

She grimaced.

But there was another issue that wouldn't leave her alone. Max thought the homeless people who came to be served a free meal at the church were dangerous criminals. That said a lot about his character.

She suddenly found herself on the verge of tears. What was going on?

If she really thought about it, Erica had to admit that she found Max...attractive. In a way that she hadn't found anyone attractive in a very long time. Maybe she'd been hoping that at some point, after this was all over—if it was *ever* all over—there might be something between them.

But that wasn't going to happen. Not after that comment.

It had been all she could do to hold her tongue when he'd said that.

"What's going on with you?" Brandon demanded as he entered her office.

Erica jumped, startled. "What do you mean?"

He leaned over the desk opposite her, his green eyes fiery with concern. "First the car wreck, then getting shot at?"

She sighed and looked at her brother. A handsome man with the same auburn hair and green eyes she had, he was just two years older than her twenty-eight years.

On the outside, he exuded charm and confidence. Underneath, she knew he was hurting, his self-esteem suffering from the blow of his fiancée ditching him for another man. And yet the experience had brought them closer together. They'd both been left by people they'd loved, and Erica was able to help him with his pain.

"I'm not sure what's going on, Brandon." She spun a pen between her fingers. "I was chasing down a lead on Molly when this all happened." She paused and looked in his eyes. "It was Peter's car, Brandon."

"What?" He frowned and slid into the chair opposite her desk.

"But I don't think it was Peter driving. The first incident, where his car sideswiped us, I might be able to put the blame on him. He's irresponsible and not thinking straight these days. But the gunfire..." She shook her head. "No way."

"Peter's been acting crazy for the past several months, but you're right, he wouldn't shoot at you. What reason would he have?"

"I don't know. I would have thought if he was going to shoot me, it would have been three years ago when I named him as a possible suspect in Molly's kidnapping." Pain at the memory made her shudder. She cleared her throat. "I'm hoping the cops can find his car and figure out who stole it."

"This is scary, sis. I don't want you going anywhere by yourself until this is resolved."

"But that's the problem. I don't know what *this* is. If I don't even know what—or who—I'm fighting, how can I win?"

"Good point." He stretched his neck and sighed. "The best thing you can do right now is to make sure you do the smart thing." He paused. "Like don't go into dangerous neighborhoods. By yourself."

She flushed. "I know that was dumb. I'm not going to do anything like that again."

"Good." He clasped his hands in front of him and leaned forward. "I got an anonymous tip on that seven-year-old kidnapped by her dad. I raided the cash box and I'm going to follow up on the tip."

She frowned. "Be careful and take Jordan with you." Sometimes tipsters were willing to meet in person if they needed some cash but it wasn't the safest way to do business.

"What time are you leaving?"

She shrugged. "You know me. I don't keep set hours."

"I'll be back by five thirty to pick you up. If you want to leave earlier, call me. If I'm not ready, I'll make arrangements."

"Fine." She rolled her eyes at her brother but she supposed letting him pick her up was the smart thing to do.

Jordan knocked on the door. "I wasn't invited to the meeting?"

Brandon motioned him in and then filled him in on the events of the morning. Erica watched the two men. Jordan was a mystery—a man with a mysterious past, but a man she'd come to trust. Even Brandon, who'd gone to high school and later college with Jordan, didn't know the secrets that haunted his friend's gray eyes.

Erica didn't press the issue. Jordan was trustworthy and good at his job, and that was all that mattered to her.

Right now, a red flush covered his cheeks and his narrowed eyes shot sparks. "Who'd want to shoot at you?"

"I was just telling Brandon I have no idea." She rubbed her eyes. "And it could have been Max the person was aiming for. He was with me for both incidents."

"You definitely need to take extra precautions," Brandon said.

"I'm planning on it."

"And if this Max guy is a trouble magnet, you need to stay away from him."

Erica pointed toward the door. "Go meet your informant. I'll keep you posted on what time I want to leave."

The two men left, muttering about how they were going to come up with a plan to protect her, and Erica turned back to her computer. She was concerned, of course, and would take precautions, but she wasn't going to let anything stop her from doing her job.

Or finding her daughter.

Time passed as she worked. Her growling stomach finally reminded her she hadn't eaten a whole lot today and it was well past supper time. Thunder rumbled in the distance and she figured there'd be rain soon.

Rachel popped into the office. "I'm out of here. There's a storm brewing out there."

"I know…I heard the thunder. I'll be fine. See you tomorrow."

"Sure." Rachel started to leave, then came back, her brow creased. Erica tilted her head. "Something on your mind?"

Rachel played with the hem of her shirt, then said, "I'm just concerned about you."

"About what?"

Rachel stared at her. "About the fact that you were in a car wreck? And you were shot at? Does the list go on?"

"Oh. That."

"Yes. That."

"I'm okay, Rachel. Really."

Rachel eyed her, doubt in her eyes. Rachel finally sighed. "Is someone making sure you get home safe?"

"Brandon said he'd be back around five thirty." She glanced at the clock and frowned. "He's late. Has he called?"

"No."

Erica waved her cousin on. "I'll call him and let him know I'll be ready to leave around six thirty." Still Rachel hesitated. "What is it, Rach?"

"I saw your mom yesterday."

Erica froze. "You did?"

"Yes. I ran into her at the grocery store."

"How was she?"

Rachel shrugged. "She seemed fine. Still working long hours at the hospital."

"Did she ask about me?"

"Yes. Said she wants to see you."

Erica felt a pang of something she couldn't identify. She and her mother had never been close—in fact, Erica had never truly felt that she mattered to her mother that much. But things had gotten worse since Molly's disappearance, and Erica knew that was her fault. She'd pulled away from her family after Molly disappeared. Her obsession with finding her daughter had been her priority. She regretted that now. "What does she want to see me about?"

"Something about putting her family back together."

"You're sure?" Erica asked, stunned.

Rachel shrugged. "That's what she said. I told her I'd tell you to call her."

"Right." And she would call her. Just like she did once or twice a month. And she'd leave a message her mother might or might not return. Just like she did once or twice a month. Her mother harbored anger with Erica and her choices and that was her way of letting Erica know it. "Well, thanks for the message."

"Sure." Rachel still hovered in the doorway. "Are you working on Molly's case tonight?"

"I am."

"Do you want me to stay and help?"

Erica shook her head. "No, I don't know how much more I'm going to be able to do anyway."

"Okay." Rachel still hesitated.

"What's up with you, Rachel? Is there something we need to talk about?"

Her cousin blinked and gave a nervous laugh. "What do you mean?"

She'd been thinking about their relationship for a while. She missed the closeness they'd shared as teens and even adults before she'd married and had a child.

"I mean ever since Molly disappeared, things have been a little strained between us. Why?"

Rachel lifted her chin a notch. "Because you pushed me away."

Erica stared, openmouthed. "I did?"

Her cousin's face hardened. "It doesn't matter now."

Erica stood. "Yes, it does. Tell me."

Finally, Rachel blurted, "You were so determined to find Molly, and I understood that. I wanted to help. I hounded you about helping and you tossed aside my offers like they weren't important, and yet for those three weeks after Molly disappeared, you spent hours upon hours with Denise Tanner. I'm family…I wanted to help. Denise was just a friend, and it seemed to me she wasn't helping as much as she was hindering, keeping you from family who wanted to—" She stopped herself and waved a hand.

Erica blinked as she processed what her cousin was saying. And then gulped when she realized she couldn't refute it. She stood. "Oh, Rachel, I didn't realize…I didn't know. I'm so sorry you felt that way."

Rachel grimaced. "I'm going home before I say anything else. I just want to see you happy, not crushed when new leads lead nowhere." For the first time in forever, Rachel wrapped her arms around Erica and gave her a squeeze. "Have a good night."

Erica cherished the embrace for a few moments then pushed back to look into her cousin's eyes. "Let's start over. Can we do that?"

Rachel sniffed then sighed. "Maybe." A smile trembled on her lips. "I want to."

"Then let's get some girl time on the calendar soon."

Rachel nodded. "Get this mess with Lydia and Max wrapped up, and we'll see what we can do."

She left, and Erica tossed the pen onto the desk and swiveled around to look out the window. She felt lighter, less burdened at the new beginning with Rachel. Erica knew Rachel was worried about her and her obsession with finding Molly, but there was nothing she could do to ease her cousin's mind in that respect. This was her life now, and until Molly came home, it would continue to be her life.

However, Rachel's revelations did resonate within her.

Rachel had been jealous of Erica's time with Denise. Erica remembered that now, although she wasn't sure it had quite registered at the time. She could see Rachel's point about how she'd pushed her away, and now Erica wondered who else felt that way. Maybe Peter? Her parents definitely did. She'd have to think about that later. Right now, she was on emotion overload.

November in Spartanburg, South Carolina, meant darkness fell early. The blackness beyond the window didn't bother her. She welcomed it. Darkness had become a friend in a strange way, because it was only in the dark of the night that she allowed herself to break, to cry, to wail out her grief and beg God to bring Molly home.

She swallowed the lump in her throat and turned back to her computer. She was so close to locating a father who'd taken his five-year-old child and fled after a bitter custody battle that he'd lost. So close.

Just like she'd been so close to finding Lydia and possibly some answers about Molly's disappearance.

With a sigh, she picked up her phone and dialed her mother's number.

And left a message for her to call.

Erica kept working. By six forty-five, she was ready to go home, and wondering where her brother was.

Her phone rang and she jumped. "Hello?"

"Stop looking for her."

Erica froze. "Who is this?"

"Stop looking for her or I'll kill her."

SEVEN

Max snapped a picture of two men meeting in the restaurant across the street. His client was convinced his partner was stealing from him and passing on bid numbers so the competition could come in just under and steal the job. From the looks of things, the client might be right.

As he focused the camera and zoomed in on the handshake, his mind went to Erica James. Just thinking about her made his pulse jump a little faster. Apparently this attraction he had for her—which he'd been trying to ignore—wasn't going to just disappear.

And before he'd learned about her work with the homeless, he hadn't really wanted it to. But two facts remained: she worked with the kind of people who were responsible for his fiancée's death, and she thought Lydia had something to do with Molly's kidnapping. He had no doubt Erica would turn Lydia in to the cops the minute she tracked her down.

But Max had other plans.

Which meant putting any kind of feelings he had for Erica on hold. Maybe permanently.

Thunder rumbled and he glanced at the dark sky. He needed the rain to hold off just a little while longer.

Max lifted the camera once again and snapped as the men

ordered and continued their conversation. No money had been exchanged, but he could be patient.

He had all night.

His phone rang and he grabbed it, hoping to see Lydia's number on the screen.

No such luck. "Hey, Chris."

"Hey, you got a minute?"

"Or two."

"I looked into some of your past cases like you asked. You've got quite a history here, don't you?" he said, sounding impressed.

Max had been the star player in his two years at the precinct. He didn't let it go to his head. Some of his busts had been due to dumb luck. Or divine guidance. "I was just doing my job, Chris. What do you have for me?"

Papers rustled. "There were a couple of possibilities that I checked out and came up empty on. The only real thing that stands out is the time you busted the daughter of Judge Terrell Brown for DUI and then wouldn't be bought off."

"I'd forgotten about that."

"Brown hasn't. Neither has the daughter. I asked him about you, and it wasn't pretty."

"Can you look into that a little more?"

"I've got feelers out on his location when your incidents went down. Should know something tomorrow." He paused.

"What is it?" Max asked.

"While Brown's a candidate, I'm not seeing his hand on this one."

"Why not?" Max looked through the viewfinder and clicked.

"Instinct. It's been three and a half years since you've been on the force. Doesn't make sense for him to all of a sudden come after you now."

Max lowered the camera as his phone beeped. He looked at

the called ID—it was his client, Carl Rogers. "I have to take this call, Chris. Thanks for going to the trouble."

"Sure. Let me know if you need anything else."

"Will do."

Max clicked over to the other line. "Hi, Carl."

"Anything?"

"You may have reason to suspect Klein's selling your bids."

A curse ripped through the line and Max grimaced. "I knew it," Carl said. "There wasn't any other explanation for why we kept losing jobs. What an idiot. Did he think I wouldn't catch on?"

"I don't have irrefutable proof, but you'll have some pictures to show Klein and ask for an explanation."

"I'll be looking for them."

Max hung up and glanced at the clock. As he lifted his camera, his thoughts went right back to Erica—before he remembered that he'd decided to put his feelings on hold.

It was going to be a long evening.

Erica couldn't move. Her brain almost couldn't process the call.

Then she flew into action.

Fingers clicked on the keyboard, activating the tracing software. She might be able to pull the number. And once she had the number she would know where it came from. Minutes later, she had it. And a few more clicks told her the location.

The caller had used a pay phone. A pay phone across the street from her office.

She jumped up and made it to the door before she stopped. Even though she had her gun with her, she couldn't go barreling out there.

One moment, she felt sure the caller had been talking about Molly, the next moment she was full of doubt. Was the caller one of the many pranksters who had complicated the investigation with false sightings and bogus reports? Or was the caller making a legitimate threat?

Or was the call even about Molly? It could be about Lydia.

Despite her fear, hope flamed anew. If the call *was* about Molly, then Molly was still alive.

She grabbed the nearest phone and called Katie. After hearing Erica's story, the detective said, "I know how much you want to believe she's still alive. I do, too, but the fact of the matter is, with the resurgence of publicity about Molly's kidnapping, we're getting the crazies calling again."

Erica bit her lip. "I know, but this was different. The person just said to stop looking for her or he would kill her. Katie, that means she might still be alive."

"If that person was for real." Katie paused. "I'll look into it, but please, Erica, don't get your hopes up."

"My hope is in the Lord, Katie. You know that."

The detective sighed. "I know. And that's exactly where it needs to be. But…"

"It's okay. Just see if you can figure out who called me."

"I'll get right on it. Was the voice male or female?"

"I thought it was male, but I don't know. It was low, harsh, like the person was using something to disguise it."

"All right, let me see what I can find out."

When she hung up, Erica dialed Brandon's number.

No answer. Jordan's number went to voice mail, too. She frowned. Where were those guys? Worry bit at her.

Max. She should call Max.

She grimaced at the thought. After his reaction to her volunteer work, she wasn't sure she wanted to see him again just yet. Then again, she didn't want to leave the office alone and possibly place herself in danger. And he *was* a P.I. If anyone could help her figure out who had called her, it was probably him.

He answered on the second ring. "Hello?"

"Hi, Max, I'm at my office. Alone. I just got a very strange call and don't want to—" She sighed. "How far are you from my office? I sure could use some help."

"I'm about fifteen minutes away. A strange call? What kind of strange call?" His concern touched her, his tone conveying that he held no grudge toward her. And she found she held none toward him. He just needed to be educated.

"Brandon was supposed to meet me at five thirty and he hasn't shown up. I'm a little worried about him, but I promised I wouldn't leave the office by myself because of everything that's happened. I know it's a bit of an inconvenience, but—"

"I'll be right there."

Relief washed over her as she heard his engine starting up. "Thanks."

She headed back to her office to try to reach Brandon or Jordan again. As she sat at her desk, she listened to the creaks and groans of the building. The heating unit hummed quietly and rain pattered against her window.

Still, neither Brandon nor Jordan answered her calls.

She stared at the phone and whispered a prayer for their safety. Then her mind went back to the anonymous caller who wanted her to stop searching for Molly.

It had to be Molly, right?

No, not necessarily. It could actually be about any of the cases she was working right now. She mentally ran down her list. The call could easily be about the little girl whose father had snatched her three weeks ago. Her heart dipped a bit at the thought, but her gut was telling her the call had to do with Molly.

Was that just because she desperately wanted to believe?

Erica rubbed the heels of her palms against her eyes and sighed. *Please, God...*

A crack of thunder made her jump. The lights flickered then went out.

Eerie silence surrounded her. Her heart pumped faster. "It's just the storm, Erica." She stepped to the window and let her eyes adjust to the darkness. She could see the lightning flashing, hear the rain coming harder. "Come on, Max, where are you?"

Erica saw headlights in the distance. They passed her office. She grabbed her purse and moved to the front door.

Lightning flashed again, illuminating a dark silhouette standing in front of the glass door. Erica screamed and dropped her purse.

The figure at the door ducked before Erica could get a glimpse of a face and hurried from the building. Erica gasped, breathless from fear. Shaky fingers checked the lock, and then Erica slid to the floor, her legs refusing to hold her anymore.

Headlights cut through the lobby, and Erica felt her pulse speed even faster. Then she recognized Max's truck and allowed herself to wilt back against the wall for a brief moment of thanks.

With effort, she rose and unlocked the door.

Max was already out of the truck, running toward her through the drenching rain. "Are you okay? Why were you sitting on the floor?"

To her surprise, she found she wanted nothing more than for Max Powell to wrap his arms around her and let her simply rest her head on his very broad shoulder. Only the memory of his reaction to her volunteer work held her back. That, and the fact that she'd only known him a short time.

And his sister possibly having something to do with Molly's kidnapping.

Erica straightened her shoulders, took a step back and told herself to be strong. She allowed him to escort her to the truck as he held his jacket above her head to keep her from getting wet, and then help her up into the seat. "It's a long story."

He climbed into the driver's side, slammed the door and turned to her. "What happened?"

"The lights went out. I was watching for you from my office window and saw your headlights. I went to wait for you in the lobby and when the lightning flashed—" she swallowed hard "—there was someone standing in front of the door. Nearly gave me a heart attack."

"Did the person say or do anything?"

"No. When I screamed, he ran."

"Ran? Did he get in a car?"

"No. Just ran through the rain toward the street. It was weird."

A frown creased his forehead. "Everything that's happening is weird."

"And now Brandon and Jordan aren't answering my calls. I'm worried something's wrong." She ran a hand over her hair. "Could you pull into that convenience store across the street? That's where the call originated from."

He lifted a brow. "How do you know?"

"I have tracing software."

"Handy," he said as he pulled out of the parking lot. A minute later, he turned right into the convenience store, and Erica jumped out of the vehicle.

She found the pay phone in the back toward the restrooms. A security camera attached to the side of the building gave her a rush of hope—could it be that easy to figure out who had called her? She stepped inside the store and approached the clerk, a young woman who looked to be in her early twenties.

"Help you?" The woman snapped her gum and swiped the counter with a cloth. Her tag read Doreen.

"Yes. I have a strange request, Doreen."

"Probably not so strange. You wouldn't believe some of the stuff that goes on around here."

"I'd like to see the security video of the pay phone and restrooms back there."

Doreen lifted a brow. "Okay, now that's strange enough. What for?"

"I got a threatening phone call and it came from that pay phone."

"You a cop?"

"I specialize in finding people. I could probably get a court order to look at the video but I really don't want to do that."

"Well, I'd show it to you, but it's broke."

"Broken?"

"Yep, got hit by lightning last night. Waiting on the repair guy to come sometime tomorrow. Sorry."

Of course. "What about the one that monitors the gas pumps. I could see who came into the store, right?"

"I reckon."

"You know how to work the video?"

"Sure. Someone tried to rob the place about three months ago and I had to show the cops the tape." Uncertainty creased the girl's brow. "But I can't leave the front untended."

"What time do you close?"

She snickered. "We don't."

Erica did her best to rein in her impatience. "Could you just put a sign on the door and say you'll be back in ten minutes?"

The young woman hesitated. In desperation, Erica said, "I'll give you twenty bucks."

"Make it fifty and you've got a deal."

"Everything all right?"

Erica turned to find Max. "Yes, Doreen here is going to show us the video footage from around the time the call was made." She passed the money to the woman who quickly slid it in her pocket.

Doreen locked the doors and put a sign in the window, and

Erica and Max followed her to the back room. "What time do you need to see?"

Erica said, "Try around seven fifteen."

Doreen clicked on the computer and within seconds had the video rolling. Erica leaned in and watched. At seven twenty-two, a figure in a hoodie walked into the store. The figure immediately reminded her of Lydia, but she didn't want to jump to conclusions. They watched a few more minutes, but Erica knew this was the person who'd made that call. "Can you back it up?"

She watched the footage again and Max said, "Can't tell anything about him."

"Or her," Erica murmured.

He shot her a dark look. "According to where he hit on the height of the door, he's around five foot five or six. It's hard to tell by body build—he's hunched over, avoiding the camera. Which means he might be quite a bit taller, too."

Erica had Doreen rewind and she watched again.

Max sighed. "I don't think you're going to get anything else from this. We need to find another camera." She told him about the nonworking camera. He shook his head. "Doreen, did you notice anything about this individual?"

She shrugged. "Nothing that caught my eye. Noticed he kept his hood pulled low and he was kinda skinny. Like a junkie. He just used the pay phone and went on his way. Didn't even come inside."

Max sighed. "Then I'd say we're done here."

Erica agreed. She thanked Doreen and followed Max to the door.

The rain had slackened to a drizzle by the time they headed back to Max's truck. She pulled out her phone once more. "I need to try Brandon—"

Her phone rang just as the words left her lips. "Brandon, are you all right?"

"Actually, this is Jordan, and yeah, Brandon's all right. He's in the hospital, though, getting patched up."

"What? What happened?"

"His informant was followed, and Brandon caught a bullet."

Erica gasped. "Where were you?"

"Grabbing the kid."

Her heart jumped. "So she's safe?"

"And back with her mama in an emergency shelter. The cops are talking to Christine there now."

Christine. The sweet young mother who'd been terrorized by her husband. When she'd left him, he'd tracked her to a hotel room and nearly killed her. He'd snatched their seven-year-old daughter and gone on the run. Now, after three months, mother and daughter were reunited and hopefully could rest assured that the terror was over.

Erica closed her eyes and breathed a brief prayer of thanks. "And Brandon's going to be all right?"

"Yeah. It's just a flesh wound. Shouldn't slow him down much."

Erica swallowed hard. "Okay, thanks for the update. I'll be at the hospital in a few minutes."

"You don't need to come. We're almost done here."

"He's my brother. I'm coming."

"You need me to pick you up?"

"No. I'm with Max."

He paused. "You're seeing a lot of him, aren't you?"

"We're looking for Molly, Jordan." Max glanced over at her, and she said, "Look, I've got to go. I'll be there shortly. Would you please put Brandon on the phone?"

Max made a U-turn to head for the hospital. Her heart gave a grateful thud at his thoughtfulness. She waited for Brandon to pick up the phone, feeling sick to her stomach with worry.

"Hey, sis, I'm all right."

"You got shot, Brandon." She hated the shakiness in her voice, but the thought of him being in danger scared her. "I know you're talking to me, but are you sure you're all right?"

"Once again, I'm fine. I'll be out of here in a few minutes. Jordan will drive me home. Sorry I didn't answer the phone, I was a little preoccupied."

"I know. I'm on the way to the hospital. We'll talk about that when I get there."

"What? No way. Don't waste your time. I'm almost ready to walk out of the door."

"But—"

"I said no, sis."

She bit her lip. "Brandon, you got shot. I can't just go home and sleep."

"That's exactly what you're going to do. You can check on me tomorrow. I'm going to take a painkiller and go to bed."

"Jordan's going to be with you, right?"

"Probably wouldn't be able to pry him from my side with a crowbar," he muttered. "He's worse than a mother hen."

She almost smiled. Almost. "All right. I'll check on you tomorrow then." She hung up with Brandon and said to Max, "You can do another U-turn." He did.

"I'm glad he's all right," Max said.

"I am, too. He didn't want me coming to the hospital."

"Doesn't want to be mothered, I guess."

She pursed her lips, trying not to be overwhelmed by emotion as she thought of her brother in the hospital with a gunshot wound.

Max didn't say anything, just reached over and grasped her cold fingers.

They rode in silence until they reached her driveway.

When he released her hand, she wanted to grab it back, to hold on to the security and warmth he offered. Instead, she curled her fingers around the handle. "Thanks for the ride."

"Anytime."

Weariness eating at her, Erica opened the car door and stopped as Max placed a hand on her arm.

"I'm also glad you called me tonight."

She lifted her gaze to his. "Even after I bit your head off earlier?"

"Even after."

"So what *was* that all about?"

He dropped his head for a moment. When he looked up, he said, "I've had more than one bad experience with the homeless. I'm embarrassed to admit this, but I suppose I'm a bit prejudiced against them." He gripped the steering wheel until his knuckles turned white. "It's not something I'm proud of. In fact, I really don't like that part of myself, but I'm not sure how to get past it."

"I…see." She didn't really. Didn't most cops have run-ins with homeless people on a regular basis? "Sounds personal."

"Very."

She closed her door. "Want to tell me about it?"

His lips tightened. "Two years ago, my fiancée was killed by a homeless man."

Erica felt her anger toward him dissolve. "Oh, no! I'm so sorry."

"Ever since then—" He shook his head as though to dislodge the memory. "I know it's wrong to lump people into one category because of one person's actions, but I can't seem to stop doing it. Tracy was a trusting woman. A woman who never met a stranger and was kind to everyone who crossed her path." He glanced at her. "Kind of like you."

Erica swallowed. "I don't know what to say," she whispered. "My heart breaks for you."

"I've let Tracy go. She's with the Lord. And while I selfishly wish she wasn't, it is what it is. I'm still here and I still have a life to live." He traced a finger down her cheek and she shivered. He smiled but it didn't reach his eyes. "Anytime you need something, don't hesitate, all right?"

She nodded and blinked back tears. "All right."

"Good. Now what time should I pick you up in the morning?"

She stared as her brain scrambled to switch gears. "Oh, my car. Right. How about eight?"

"I'll be here."

"Do you think Mrs. Harrison would let us see Lydia's room first thing in the morning?"

"Lydia doesn't have a room there anymore, but I'll ask if she minds me bringing you by and introducing you."

"Great." Erica looked at her dark house and shivered. She'd forgotten to leave some lights on. Again.

"You want me to walk you in?"

She gave a breathless little laugh that sounded more scared than confident. "No. I'll be all right. I'm just a little spooked after everything that's happened in the last twenty-four hours."

"Who could blame you?"

In the close quarters of the car, she looked him in the eye. "Thanks again for coming to the rescue, Max."

His eyes dropped to her lips then rose back to meet her gaze. Thanks to the streetlight, she could make out the hue of a red flush on his cheeks. "Sure. I'll just wait here until you get inside."

On impulse, she leaned in and gave him a quick hug. "I'll see you in the morning."

She opened the door and raced for the cover of her front porch. From the rocker to her left, a shadow rose. Erica stepped back with a scream.

EIGHT

Max bolted from the car as he snatched his weapon from his shoulder holster and trained it on the figure that had stepped toward Erica from the shadows. "Hey! Back away!"

The shadow froze, and Erica darted back into the rain toward Max.

"Erica! It's me, Peter."

Max grabbed her hand and led her back onto the porch, out of the rain. "Are you crazy? Scaring her like that?"

Peter held his hands up as though in surrender. "I thought she saw me."

"Nobody saw you," Max growled.

"I'm sorry. I was practically asleep when you drove up."

"What are you doing here?" Erica asked. Max could feel the tension vibrating from her.

Her brother swiped a hand down his face. "The cops think I had something to with crashing into you today. They think I was responsible for that hit-and-run, and the shooting."

"They said they didn't have any proof," Erica said.

"They don't." The man fidgeted, fingers tapping against his leg. "But they're looking for it. It's only a matter of time."

"Only a matter of time before what?" Max felt himself leaning toward Peter as if to drive him back, away from Erica.

He told himself to cool it. He put his protective instincts on hold and said, "I thought you had an alibi."

Peter snorted and sank back onto the rocker, his leg jiggling up and down. "I did, but my alibi seems to have suffered some memory loss." Sarcasm dripped from his words. He grabbed Erica's hand. "Erica, you've got to believe I didn't have anything to do with that. I would *never* hurt you." His vehemence was almost believable.

Erica sighed and unlocked the door. "Let's get inside where it's warm. It's freezing and you're soaking wet."

Peter bolted to his feet as though sitting was too much for him. They stepped inside and he hesitated. "Can I have a towel?"

Max noticed the shivers trembling through the man's body. Erica set her purse on the small table just inside the foyer and went to the bathroom off the hall. Lips tight, she handed Peter the towel. "How did you get here?"

"I walked."

Erica flinched and Max raised a brow. She said, "That's a good ten miles, Peter. Are you crazy?"

The man shrugged.

Max asked, "Where were you tonight around seven?"

"On the way here. Why?"

"It wasn't him," Erica said to Max.

"What wasn't me?" His gaze darted from Max to Erica. Max thought his eyes looked clear. He wasn't high right now, but he was jittery, constantly moving.

"Someone scared Erica at the office tonight."

Peter frowned. "Well you're right, it wasn't me." He looked toward the back bedroom then said to Erica, "Do you still have some of my clothes here?"

"Yes. Go take a shower and warm up. I'll fix some coffee."

"Decaf, okay?" He started down the hall then turned back. "Oh, I meant to tell you, I saw Denise Tanner today."

Erica blinked. "You did? When?"

His brow crinkled. "Right before I left to come over here. I was at the gas station trying to get someone to buy me a soda and she pulled in." He rubbed his head and smirked. "I think she tried to avoid me, but I didn't let her. Stepped right in front of her and asked her what she was doing in town."

"And you wonder why she never cared much for you. You constantly antagonized the woman."

He shrugged his apathy. "She always looked down her nose at me. She was the bossiest thing ever, and I didn't like her. But apparently her father is on his deathbed. Not expected to live much longer."

"Oh, no. I knew he was sick, but I didn't know that he was close to death." Erica frowned. "Why didn't she call me and let me know?"

"I don't know." He raised a shaky hand. "She didn't look all that great, though. Must be taking a toll on her." He turned again and went to the room down the hall.

"Denise Tanner?" Max asked.

"I can't believe this. I just talked to her last week. She said her father was declining, but she didn't say anything about coming this way."

"Maybe it was really sudden." Max saw her glance at her phone and figured she wanted to call her friend. "I'll get out of here. Are you sure you'll be all right with him here?"

"Yes. Peter's not the one after me."

Max pursed his lips and thought about it. "We don't know that for sure."

Erica placed her hands on her hips. "Well, I do."

Max gave a slow nod. "Just like I know Lydia wouldn't be involved in a kidnapping." Erica's face flushed. "Call me if you need anything else tonight, promise?"

She nodded. "I promise. I really appreciate your help."

"Anytime." He stepped onto the porch. "At least the rain's stopped."

As Max walked down the steps, movement to his right caught his attention. He froze and squinted toward the dark shadows. "Who's there?"

The shadow darted around the corner of the house. Max chased after it.

"Max?" He could hear Erica calling after him, but had no time to stop and fill her in.

"Stay in the house!"

Within a second, Max was around the side of the house and staring into inky blackness. The neighborhood streetlights didn't reach back far enough to illuminate the area behind the house and the quarter moon wasn't any help, either.

The light drizzle turned to a downpour again. Old cop instincts humming, Max pulled his weapon from his holster and clicked the safety off. Moving forward, eyes probing, he listened. A footstep to his left? He whirled, gun ready.

A figure slithered behind a tree. He moved toward it, rounding the tree with his gun outstretched. Nothing.

Heart hammering with adrenaline coursing through him, he placed his back against the tree and waited. Silence. The cold began to settle in his bones. His toes turned numb. For ten minutes, he stood in the dark, listening, hearing nothing but the night sounds.

In his mind, he pictured the person using the same strategy—holding still and silent, waiting for Max to make the first move.

"Max?"

Erica.

He kept the gun in his hand but lowered it as he heard her approaching. "Max, are you all right? Answer me."

Max kept his eyes glued to the area around him. He saw nothing. Heard nothing.

"I'm here, Erica."

He ground his teeth in frustration and walked toward her, keeping his senses tuned to anything out of the ordinary. As he approached, he saw the weapon in her hand. "He's gone."

"Who's gone? You scared me when you took off like that."

"I told you to stay in the house."

"And I don't sit back and wait very well when someone's in danger because of me." Together, they walked back to the house. Max glanced over his shoulder, feeling like he and Erica were one big bull's-eye.

Once they reached the porch, she asked, "What did you see?"

He pointed. "Someone was trying to look in that window."

She spun to her left. "That's my bedroom window."

He opened the door. "Is Peter still here?"

"I'm still here." Peter walked out, fresh from the shower. He looked much better, and seemed entirely oblivious to what had just happened. "I'm going to get something to eat if that's all right."

"Yeah. Sure." She waved him into the kitchen.

Once Peter disappeared around the corner, Max asked, "Do you have an alarm system?"

"Yes."

"Turn it on, okay?"

"Of course." She crossed her arms in a self-hug and shivered. "I think Peter's going to end up staying here tonight."

Max reached out and rubbed her arms, trying to chase away her chill. Then he surprised himself by pulling her into a gentle hug. And she surprised him by letting him do it. The feel of her in his arms felt right. Like something that was meant to be. Without letting go, he asked, "You think Peter'll be sober enough to help you if you need it?"

She pulled away from him and blew out a breath as she

glanced out into the night. "I don't know. Maybe whoever it was won't be back."

Max wasn't sure he agreed and mentally reviewed a plan to make sure Erica was safe tonight. In the meantime, he'd hold on to the memory of what it felt like to hold her next to his heart—and pray he had the opportunity to do it again.

Erica shut the door, her hand still on the knob, the feel of Max's embrace a strong sensation. Within the circle of his arms, she'd felt safe. Comforted. She wanted to beg him not to go, ask him to hold her and—

She heard Peter in the kitchen. Wanting something she couldn't have would get her nowhere. Max was off-limits.

At least for now.

She walked into the kitchen. "Are you staying here tonight?" She wasn't quite sure whether she wanted him to or not.

He looked up from the refrigerator, an apple in his left hand. "Do you mind?"

"No." She bit her lip then said, "I want to help you, Peter."

"Why? You still think I had something to do with Molly's disappearance." His bitterness filled the air. "Why would you want to help someone who could do such an awful thing?"

Erica blinked. "No, I don't. You were cleared."

"But you doubted," he said. "You really thought I would do something so vile as to kidnap my own niece—" He waved a hand and a deep sadness entered his eyes. "Never mind."

"Well, what was I supposed to think?" she demanded. "You came to me only a few weeks before, begging for money to shoot up your arm or snort up your nose. You shoved me against the wall when I refused and you raided my wallet for a lousy twenty bucks." Anger at the memory crested. She stepped forward and jabbed a finger in his chest. He flinched while she continued. "And you told me if I didn't give you

what you wanted, you'd find a way to get it. What was I supposed to think?"

She couldn't stop the sob that broke free.

Erica whirled and went into the den. She sank onto the
couch and tried to get a grip on her emotions even as tears
ran freely down her cheeks.

Peter followed her, jaw tight, eyes narrowed. "I don't remember that."

"Well, you were high. It's not surprising you don't remember." She swiped the tears and sniffed.

"I'm going to go." He started for the door.

"That's right, Peter. Run away. Because that's always
worked so well for you."

He turned on her. "Look, Erica, you don't understand…
you…" He stopped and dropped his head. "This isn't why I
came here tonight. I wanted to apologize for earlier."

"For what?"

"For letting Polo follow me here the other night. For whatever's going on that would make someone steal my car and
try to frame me for hurting you. For—" he threw his hands
out "—for whatever I need to apologize for."

Erica stared at her brother. "What is this, Peter? You're
acting strange."

His eyes changed, hardened, yet the conflicted sadness
remained. "Because I offered you an apology? What do you
want from me?"

"I want you to go to rehab and quit destroying your life!"

"Maybe I want to destroy it so you'll quit trying to run it."
He took a deep breath and closed his eyes. When he opened
them, she thought she saw a sheen of tears there. But before
she could question him, he strode to the front door, opened
it and walked out into the night.

"Peter, wait!"

But he was already heading down the street, his phone

pressed to his ear, shoulders hunched against the cold. "Come back!" He ignored her. Within five minutes, a car pulled up beside him and Peter climbed in. The vehicle roared to the stop sign at the end of the street and turned right. She had no hope of getting him to come back now.

Erica dropped her face into her hands and let the sobs come.

Two minutes later, a knock disrupted her crying jag. Rising to her feet, she snagged the gun from the top drawer of the desk and peered out the window.

Max.

She opened the door. "Why did you come back?"

His eyes swept her face. "I never left. I thought you might need me." He shut the door.

Her lower lip trembled. "I'm fine." She set the gun on the foyer table and gave her wet face an angry swipe.

"Sure you are."

His sympathy undid her. The sobs broke free once again and he pulled her into his arms. At first Erica wasn't quite sure what to think, but the blessed feeling of comfort washed over her and she hung on to it until she was able to rein in the tears.

When she opened her eyes, she found herself snuggled against Max's chest and sitting on the couch. Embarrassed that she didn't realize he'd led her there, she pulled away and scrubbed her eyes. "I'm so sorry."

"What for?"

"For blubbering all over you. I barely know you." She hiccuped and sniffed. "But thanks for the shoulder. I needed it."

He smiled. "Jordan is outside watching your house. He and I are taking shifts. Brandon tried to insist on helping, but the pain meds were kicking."

"Poor Brandon." The ever-present guilt tugged at her.

"He'll be all right. I asked for the four-to-eight shift so I could take you to get your car in the morning." He paused. "And talk you into breakfast again."

Erica sighed and pressed her fingertips against her eyelids, hoping to relieve some of the pressure. "Thanks. I appreciate that."

For the second time that night, Max moved to the door. "See you in a few hours. Get some rest if you can."

Erica nodded. "I'll do my best."

Erica leaned against the door as she turned the lock. A quick check out the window showed Max driving away and Jordan on guard.

She shook her head at the thought that someone wanted to hurt her. Who? A disgruntled spouse who was sitting in jail for kidnapping because she'd caught up with him? An angry ex-spouse who now had to pay child support? Any number of people had a bone to pick with her, but no one really stood out in her mind.

Stop searching for her or I'll kill her. The caller's words still echoed in her ears and Erica couldn't help but wonder, if she kept searching for her daughter, would that lead to Molly's death?

Would it lead to her *own* death?

NINE

At eight o'clock Thursday morning, Max felt a dart of pleasure at the sight of Erica stepping out of her house and walking toward him. In jeans and a sweater, with her auburn hair pulled up in a neat ponytail, she looked comfortable, peaceful.

He wished he could say the same for his nerves. They were on edge. Probably from the gallon of coffee he'd drunk over the last three hours.

She slipped into the passenger seat. "Morning."

"Hey." He handed her a cup of coffee and a bagel. "Compliments of Brandon. He stopped by about thirty minutes ago."

"What?" She grimaced. "I wish he wouldn't push himself so hard."

"He cares about you."

"I know. He's a good brother. I just wish he would take it easy sometimes."

"Yeah. Like you do, right?"

She stuck her tongue out at him and he laughed. He swallowed a bite of the bagel and took a sip of coffee. "Bea agreed to meet us at eight thirty. She has a doctor's appointment at ten."

"That works for me. Did you get any rest last night?"

"A bit. You?"

"A bit."

Which meant not much. "Did you get hold of your friend, Denise?"

She winced. "No. I didn't even try. I plan to as soon as we're finished with Mrs. Harrison."

Max kept his mouth shut, but thought if a woman Erica considered her best friend hadn't bothered to call and let her know she was in town, then maybe she needed a new best friend. Like him, maybe.

"I appreciate you arranging this."

He shrugged. "I've been by to see Bea several times in the last few days and the story is always the same. She hasn't seen Lydia but will call if she does."

Erica played with her napkin, and he could almost see her thinking. "Well, I haven't talked to her," she said. "I want to see what she has to say to me."

He had a feeling it wouldn't be anything new, but he supposed she needed to hear it herself. "What makes you think she'll tell you anything different than what she's told me?"

"I don't think she will, necessarily. But I won't know until I try."

He finished off the bagel and cranked the car. "Then let's do it. She's expecting us anytime now." As he pulled away from the curb, he said, "I did some research on Lydia's calls."

"What do you mean?"

"I bought her a cell phone not too long ago and I get the bill. I went through the latest one and found something interesting."

Erica lifted a brow. "What'd you find?"

"Lydia made several phone calls to a construction company and got one return call from the same business."

"Why is that weird?"

"For someone living on the streets and doing drugs, it just struck me as kind of strange."

She nodded. "Okay, so did you call the number?"

"I did."

"And?"

"I got voice mail. We'll try again a little later. I want to know what kind of business Lydia had with them."

"Won't the cops have questioned them already?"

He shook his head. "I'm not sure. If they did, Katie didn't mention it."

"Okay, sounds good to me."

Max looked in the rearview mirror. No one followed. At least no one obvious. His mind worked the puzzle of his sister's ability to hide so well when he knew most of her hiding places.

She may have found a new one. At least, he hoped she did. Otherwise, her disappearance didn't bode well. Had Lydia escaped her attacker two nights ago only to fall into the wrong hands?

He sent up a brief prayer and a desperate plea for the Lord to keep the girl safe.

Erica watched Max's strong hands grip the wheel. She inhaled, liking his fresh, clean scent. He smelled...good. Really good. He must have showered before coming over in the wee hours of the morning. She wondered if he'd done that for her.

She thought about his loss. A fiancée. Someone he'd loved enough to want to spend the rest of his life with her.

She must have been a special woman.

And she'd been killed by a homeless person. Her heart ached for him even as it thumped a little harder at his nearness.

Her attraction to him made her frown as she watched him drive. What was she going to do with this pull she felt for him?

What *could* she do with it?

A plan formed in her mind. What if she invited him to spend some time with her at the shelter? Introduced him to some of the regulars and let him see that the man who killed his fiancée was an aberration? That the homeless man's act of murder was not the norm?

She felt sure he knew this in his head, but had a feeling his heart needed to learn it.

She watched him. He was as lost in his own thoughts as she. Warmth settled in her belly as she remembered his sweet care when she'd cried on his shoulder. Longing swept through her—oh, to have that on a daily basis. To have someone next to her, someone in her life to support and offer support in return.

That would be so wonderful.

But she couldn't have that with Max. What if his sister *was* guilty of having something to do with Molly's kidnapping? What would happen then?

She knew the answer to that.

Max would do everything in his power to help the girl stay out of jail; he would fight for her no matter what.

And Erica would be just as determined to see Lydia Powell pay for whatever part she played in the crime that had broken her heart.

Max's sister was too big of a barrier to get past.

She bit her lip and looked out the window. Max Powell might be good-looking and make her pulse pound a little faster when she was around him, but that didn't mean she could fall for him. Because when his sister was charged, he would be forced to choose sides.

And Erica had no doubt which side he would choose.

For her own sake, she needed to guard her heart.

Lydia may be innocent, a little voice whispered.

Erica ignored it. Lydia was the first thing in three years that looked like a solid lead and there was no chance she was going to let her feelings for Max Powell get in the way.

Erica would find Lydia, and find out what she knew.

No matter what.

* * *

Max pulled up to the curb of Bea Harrison's home. "She was old when Lydia lived here," he told Erica. "At least it seemed that way to me. I think she's around seventy now."

"Seventy's not that old these days." She shot him an amused glance.

He gave her a wry grin. "I have to admit, the older I get, the younger seventy seems. It wasn't too long ago I thought thirty was the equivalent of having one foot in the grave. Now I'll be thirty in three months." He shook his head and looked up to see Bea standing at the screen door. "Come on, she's waiting on us."

They climbed from the vehicle and Max hunched his shoulders against the chill. Thanksgiving would be here soon. He swallowed at the thought. Another holiday without a family of his own. This time of year sent his emotions spinning.

Anger over his childhood and grief over his fiancée surged to the surface often. Technically, he still had Lydia, but who knows if she would show up for a meal?

Or if she would even be able to come. If she was sitting in jail, or on the run, a happy family celebration would most likely be out of the question.

He sighed at his sarcasm. Focus on the positive, right?

Pushing the depressing thoughts aside, he stepped inside the warm house and introduced Erica. The two women greeted each other and Max said, "I'm still looking for Lydia, Bea. Have you seen or heard from her?"

"Have a seat, you two." The rail-thin yet spry woman didn't look seventy. Energy radiated from her and he could see Erica was drawn to her. Bea asked, "Would you like something to drink? Eat?"

Erica shook her head. "I don't care for anything, thanks."

Impatience tugged at him. He forced it away. This woman had been able to reach a part of his sister no one else had touched. He supposed he should be jealous. But he wasn't, he was just glad Lydia had someone she trusted. "Me, either, Bea. We don't have a lot of time, but I wanted to introduce Erica to you."

Bea's sharp eyes homed in on Erica. "You're Molly's mother, aren't you?"

Max saw Erica flinch, but she nodded. "Yes."

"I recognize you from your picture on the news recently. I also followed your story three years ago." She clucked her tongue. "I just couldn't believe a child could disappear from the zoo on a field trip." Her lips pursed. "I've had close to a hundred children come through my home in the last thirty years and none of 'em went missing on my watch." She narrowed her eyes. "Well, Lydia might be the exception to that. But I always knew she'd come back."

Max interrupted, hating the pain in Erica's eyes. "I know you told me on the phone that you haven't seen Lydia." He leaned forward. "Please, Bea, this is for Lydia's own good. You've been around the system enough to know that protecting her isn't going to be good for her in the long run. We need to find her."

For the first time, doubt creased her brow and she sighed. "Max, I've never had a biological child, but if I did, she would have been just like Lydia. Lydia's like my own." She paused. "I didn't get her young enough. I would have raised her better than what she had. Deep down Lydia has a good heart. She just can't seem to stop making stupid decisions."

"I know."

"And while she has her faults, she's good to me." She nodded toward her ankle, which was wrapped up in a brace. "She came by a day after I fell about a month ago and bought me this. Said I should go to the doctor, but I don't have any insurance. Yep, she's good to me."

"And you're good to her. Maybe too good." He took her hand. "You know I'd pay for any doctor visit you needed."

She flushed and waved him off. "I know that, but I knew it was just a sprain and would heal in time."

Max leaned back. "Look at it this way. We want to find Lydia because we want to help her. Someone may be after her, and I want to find her first." He gripped her hand. "Please, Bea, tell me what you know."

The woman twisted her fingers together. "What do you mean someone's after her and wants to hurt her?" He told her about the attack they'd saved her from the other night. Bea listened, eyes wide. "You really think she's still in danger?"

"I don't know, but we're trying to find her before it's too late."

Bea closed her eyes for a moment then stood and said, "All right, I'll be right back."

As she disappeared down the hall toward the bedrooms, Erica asked in a low voice, "What makes you think Lydia is in danger, other than the attack the other night?" She shot a glance toward the hall. "I thought that was just a random thing of Lydia being in the wrong place at the wrong time."

He shrugged. "Just a feeling."

Bea's sprightly steps echoed on the hardwood as she returned to the kitchen. She set a shoe box on the table and heaved a sigh. "You're sure she's in danger? Because I promised Lydia I'd guard this with my life."

"What's in it?"

"I don't know." She huffed in indignation. "I didn't look. I just made her promise it wasn't drugs or anything that could get me arrested. She swore it wasn't."

Max lifted a brow. "And you believed her?" It wasn't like Bea to have her head in the sand. She'd had enough kids who were hooked on drugs come through her house to know how it worked. You couldn't trust them. Period. He would have looked the minute Lydia walked out the door.

Which was probably why she left the box with Bea.

Bea was nodding. "Yes. Strangely enough I did believe her about this. She said it was a memory box. She'd come by to visit it every once in a while."

They all looked at the box for a moment, and then Max reached for the lid, wondering what he was about to find, and knowing it probably wasn't going to be anything good.

Erica desperately wanted to snatch the box from the table and just dump out the contents. Instead, she curled her fingers into fists and held on to her unraveling patience as Max removed the lid.

He stared down into the box, his expression unreadable, and then pulled out a photo. Erica scooted forward to see. "That's you, isn't it?"

"Yeah." Surprise tinged his voice. "This was taken on Lydia's eighteenth birthday. She was sober and being civil to me. I took her out to eat at her favorite restaurant and the server snapped the picture." He ran his fingers over his sister's face, and Erica's heart cramped at the pain etched on his features.

He shook himself and set the picture aside to pull other items out. A cheap necklace with a heart pendant, a pack of cards, a college application. "She has dreams," Erica whispered.

"Yeah. She's wanted to be an architect for as long as I can remember." Max cleared his throat and held up a small piece of paper. "A business card." He read it and looked up. "Kenneth Harper, Brown and Jennings Construction. It's the same company that called her cell phone."

"Then they're next on the list," Erica said.

He pulled out the last item—a thick envelope. He opened the flap and reached in.

Erica gasped as he withdrew a stack of money.

Max set it on the table and stared at it. "Whoa."

"Where would she get that?" Erica asked Bea.

Bea shook her head, the dumbfounded expression leaving no doubt she was just as surprised. "She never said anything about it."

Max counted the bills. "Twenty fifty-dollar bills."

"A thousand bucks?" Erica lifted a brow.

He sat back and crossed his arms. "I have no idea where she would have gotten this kind of money."

Erica picked up another picture. "Who's this?"

Max took the picture from her and flipped it over. "It just says, 'Me and Red.'"

"Who's Red?"

Bea said, "She was in rehab with Lydia at that place across town."

"Billings Rehab Center," Max said. "I went to visit her while she was there, but she wouldn't see me. That was when she was first sent there. After I kept going back, she finally understood I wasn't going to give up and started letting me visit."

Bea nodded and told Erica, "She was court ordered to go to Billings after she was kicked out of high school for having drugs on her. She spent four months there."

Max looked at Erica, disappointment evident on his face. "It seemed to help. For a while. She started talking to me and we were working on our relationship, but then—" He shrugged. "After she got out and celebrated her eighteenth birthday, things went downhill fast."

"Do you think Red would know where Lydia is?" Erica asked.

Bea sighed. "Red's probably your best chance. She and Lydia were real close. Probably still are."

"Do you know where we can find her?"

"No. All I know is she goes by Red. I don't know her real name or where she's from. Nothing."

Max stood. "I can probably get her name from the rehab center."

"That's protected information, isn't it?" Bea frowned.

Max smiled and met Erica's eyes. "We have our ways." The smile slipped as he looked at the money. "Just keep this here for now, okay? Until we find out where she got it."

Erica shook her head. "There's no way a drug addict would have a thousand dollars tucked away. It would be gone in a split second."

"You think it's not hers?" Bea asked.

"I don't know. If it is, the reason she's holding on to it has got a stronger hold on her than the drugs."

Hope flashed in Max's eyes. "Yeah. True." He slapped the lid back on the box and stood. "Let's go see if we can find that reason."

TEN

As Max walked around to the driver's side of his truck after opening Erica's door for her, he found himself checking the road. When he settled behind the wheel, he glanced in the rearview mirror. Something was making him uneasy, but he couldn't say what. He felt watched, and he didn't like that he didn't see anyone doing the watching.

"I think that was productive," Erica said.

"Definitely." With one more glance in the mirror, he grabbed his phone and called the number for Brown and Jennings Construction. "I'll see if we can stop by and talk to Kenneth Harper."

Erica nodded. "After we talk to him, I need to go in to the office for at least a couple of hours. Rachel's already left three messages on my voice mail and it's only ten thirty."

Max drove, his mind mulling over the thousand dollars cash in the box. Where would Lydia have gotten that much money? And a thousand even? All fifty-dollar bills. He looked in the mirror. Nothing alarming caught his attention. A blue Toyota behind him. A white Honda next to him.

The phone continued to ring. Just as he was about to hang up, a harried voice answered, "Brown and Jennings."

"Could I speak to Kenneth Harper?"

"He's out at a site giving an estimate." Papers rustled in

the background. "Looks like he'll be back here around lunchtime."

"He have a cell phone?"

"Who is this?"

"I'm a private investigator trying to track down a young woman named Lydia Powell. Do you know her?"

"Nope, sorry. Name doesn't ring a bell." There was a pause, and then, "Wait a minute. Yes, it does. Isn't she the girl the cops are looking for?"

"Yes."

"Yeah, I remember seeing her name on the news. Why are you looking for her here?"

"I found your company's business card in some of her things."

"Oh. Wow. You'll have to talk to Ken. He's the owner, and if Lydia talked to anyone around here, it was probably him."

"Okay, thanks." Max hadn't held too much hope that this woman would know something, but it had been worth a shot. "So may I have the cell number?"

"Sure." She rattled it off and Max repeated it so Erica could write it down.

He hung up and tried the number. No answer. He left a message and then drove Erica to her office. Several cars filled the parking lot, including hers.

"You mind if I come in?" he asked.

"Of course not." She climbed from the truck, and then glanced behind him. "I don't think we were followed, do you?"

"I didn't see anyone, but I was wondering the same thing at Bea's house." He thought for a moment. "I'm going to call her and tell her to be on the alert."

Alarm crossed her features. "You don't think someone would try to hurt her, do you?"

"If they thought she knew something about Lydia, they

might." He frowned. "I was careful—very careful—about being followed."

"But not careful enough?"

"I'm not a hundred percent sure, and I don't like that."

He made a call to Bea, who said everything was fine but she'd keep her eyes open, and another to a buddy named Nick Kirby, who was still on the force and still a good friend. He explained what he needed and said to Erica, "Nick's going to hang out and watch Bea's house for the rest of the day and night."

Relief crossed her face. "Good. I would hate to be the reason trouble arrives on her doorstep."

He followed her into the building, trailing a few steps behind her, eyes roaming, senses tuned to the area around them. He wouldn't mind seeing her office, but the main reason he wanted to go in was to make sure there wasn't a bad surprise waiting inside for her.

He was probably just being paranoid.

But that was all right.

Inside, the warmth hit him and he shed his coat to hang it on the rack. Erica turned to the young woman at the desk and said, "Rachel, this is Max Powell."

He shook hands with the pretty receptionist and thought he saw a bit of a family resemblance. Cousins, Erica had said. "Nice to meet you."

She eyed him curiously. "You, too."

He looked around. "So, this is it, huh?"

"Yep." She smiled. "This way to my office."

"I put your mail on your desk," Rachel said.

"Thanks." Erica turned into the office three doors down. Max stepped up to help her slip her coat off. As he did, his fingers accidentally slid across the back of her neck, touching her soft skin.

She shivered and turned to look at him, surprise on her

face. He cleared his throat. "Where do you want me to hang this?"

Erica blinked and nodded to a coat rack behind the door. He hung the jacket up for her. "Nice office," he said. He practically groaned at the lameness, but right now he needed to get his mind off the way her skin had felt. Because in that moment, all of his arguments about why he should ignore his attraction to this woman had flown out the window.

"Thanks. It's nothing much, but it serves its purpose." She shifted through the messages and the mail. With a frown, she pulled an envelope from the stack. "This is weird."

"What is it?"

"It's addressed to me, but there's no return address or stamp." Erica slid her letter opener under the tab and pulled out a sheet of paper. Her face went pale and she dropped into the chair behind her desk.

"What is it?" Max asked. He stepped forward and took the paper from her. It said, "I warned you. Stop looking for her or she dies."

"The same message as my phone call last night." She rubbed a shaky hand over her eyes. "It has to be about Molly, right?"

"Or Lydia."

"But the person is warning me. You haven't gotten anything about not searching for Lydia, have you?"

He rubbed his chin. "No."

Excitement darkened her green eyes. "Molly's still alive, Max." Her throat worked and deep joy filled her face. "If she's alive, I have a chance to get her back. You can't imagine the horrible thoughts I've had about who might have taken her," she whispered.

"I can imagine. But you have to keep fighting those thoughts, praying against them." He reached over and took her hand. The fragile strength brought his protective instincts surging to the surface.

"I know. I do every day."

"And keep believing you can get her back." As soon as the words left his lips, he wondered if he should encourage her to continue hoping. Three years was a long time. Odds were completely against Erica being reunited with her child.

Odds he was sure she could quote him.

She pulled her hand from his and reached for the note and he held it aloft with thumb and forefinger. "Let's see if Katie can get anything off this."

"Fingerprints. Yes, of course. You're right." She took a deep breath and rubbed a hand down her face. "I usually think a little more clearly. It's just…"

"I get it."

She reached for the phone. He noticed she didn't have to look up Katie Randall's number. She hung up. "She's on her way over to pick it up."

As they waited, Max decided to ask Erica a question he'd had on his mind for a while. "What made you volunteer at the homeless shelter?"

She flushed. "Well, if I'm going to be honest, I'll have to admit my motives weren't completely pure at first."

Intrigued, he leaned forward. "Why do you say that?"

She picked up Molly's picture. "One of the first tips that came in was that she'd been seen at the shelter eating a free meal. No one remembered who she was with, just that she was there. The police got several calls about her being seen there so we all felt it was a legitimate tip."

"So you went there."

"I did. Of course no one would talk to me. But I noticed the rapport between the servers and the homeless. I signed up to serve the next day. It took time, but they came to trust me. I learned that Molly was there two days after she was kidnapped, but I didn't learn anything else over the next few weeks. I developed a relationship with the people there and—" she shrugged "—I stayed." She eyed him. "They're not all criminals."

"Realistically, I know that." He rubbed his chin and eyed her. "But what about the ones who are?"

She said, "I won't say I don't take precautions. Of course I do. But I've come to care for these people. I've listened to their stories. And shared mine. I'm not homeless, but 'there but for the grace of God, go I,' you know?"

"Yeah. I know." And he did. He understood what she meant.

"Why don't you come with me? Help me serve? Meet the people?"

An outright refusal hovered on his tongue, but the look on her face kept him from expressing it.

A knock on the door made them both jump. Relieved he didn't have to answer right away, Max turned to see Brandon in the doorway. Erica hopped to her feet and rushed to her brother. "Are you all right? What are you doing here?"

"I'm all right. Feeling a bit rough, but I had a new case I wanted to get the paperwork on." He held up a hand to halt her protests. "I can't just sit around doing nothing."

Jordan stepped into the room behind his friend and lifted his brow when he caught sight of Max. "You're becoming a regular fixture, aren't you?"

Max remembered that when they'd first met, Brandon had made a reference to Jordan as Erica's boyfriend. And while Erica quickly set the record straight, it appeared that Jordan might have a different take than Erica.

He was surprised by the spike of jealousy he suddenly felt.

Max met Jordan's stare head-on. "I'm doing what I can to help."

Rachel entered the crowded office. "Detective Randall is here."

Hope flared in Erica's eyes. "Show her in, please."

"What's she doing here?" Brandon asked as Rachel went to get the detective. His color had paled just since entering the office. Erica must have noticed as she waved him into a chair. "Sit down before you fall down."

Brandon didn't argue.

Jordan took the other seat and left Max standing.

"Katie's here because someone sent a letter with a rather cryptic message," Erica explained. "I want her to take a look at it."

"What kind of message?" Brandon asked.

Max's phone buzzed and he pulled it from his pocket. "It's the guy from the construction company," he told Erica. "I'll take this outside."

Jordan watched Max very closely as he left the room. Yup, the guy definitely had his own ideas about Erica.

Ideas that Max had to admit he didn't like one bit.

Erica was torn. She wanted to hear the conversation between Max and the man on the phone, yet she knew her obligation was to Katie. She forced a smile. "Come on in."

"Good to see you again, Erica."

"You, too." Erica stepped back into her office. Jordan and Brandon both rose and offered the detective a seat. Katie took one look at Brandon and chose Jordan's. When her brother simply sat back down without protest, Erica knew he was in pain.

"What's this about someone leaving you a nasty note?" asked the detective.

Erica filled the group in on the phone call and the note. Brandon's jaw tightened as Jordan scowled. "Should have told us about this earlier."

"I didn't have time." She looked at Katie. "I think this means that Molly could still be alive. Don't you?" She could hear the desperation in her voice, but didn't care.

Katie frowned. "But, Erica, you've been actively searching for Molly since she disappeared. What's different about the search now?"

"I think this means I must be getting closer. Somebody must be feeling more threatened than they have in the past."

"About what?" Katie asked.

"Lydia Powell, maybe? I think she may know something and someone doesn't want me to find her. Maybe they're warning me off trying to find Lydia." She hated to say the words out loud, especially since Max thought his sister was completely innocent. And yet, what else was she supposed to think?

Max came back into the office and leaned against the wall. Erica picked up the note and handed it to Katie. "Will you see if you can get any prints off this?"

Katie pulled a glove from her back pocket and snapped it onto her hand. She slid the note from the envelope, read it, then returned it. "I'll see what I can do. No promises, though."

"I know."

Katie paused, looked at Erica and said, "It's okay to hope, but don't pin your emotions on this, okay?"

Erica pursed her lips then nodded. She knew Katie was right. But still, it was hard to squash that little seedling of wild hope that wanted to sprout like a wildflower.

Katie left and Brandon said, "I think you need to cool it on the search for Molly. Let Jordan and me take over."

Erica snorted. "Not likely."

"Seriously, sis. This person may not be fooling around. What if you keep searching and Molly ends up dead?"

Erica bit her lip. It was that very question that had been

tearing her up. "I think if the person wanted Molly dead, he would have killed her long before now."

"Assuming the person we're talking about is Molly," Brandon said.

Erica sighed and rubbed her eyes. "Exactly."

Max asked, "Are you up to visiting the construction site?"

"Yes, of course. When?"

He glanced at his watch. "Around two this afternoon."

"I can do that."

"We can grab a bite in the meantime."

"I can't. Unless you want to help me at the homeless shelter—I'm serving lunch today."

He stared at her for a moment. "I'll take a rain check."

Sadness pressed in on her but she forced a smile. Maybe Max just wasn't ready yet. "I understand."

"I'll sit outside and make sure you're safe while you're there."

Jordan stepped forward and put a hand on Erica's arm. "Let me go with Max to the construction site. No need to put yourself through the stress of it."

"No." She moved away from Jordan. "Molly's my daughter. If you want to help find her, I welcome it, but I won't stop searching myself. You know I've got to go to the site." She softened her tone. "But thanks for the offer."

Jordan's nostrils flared, but he backed away. He studied her for a moment longer, compassion in his angry gaze.

At least she hoped it was compassion and not pity. As Erica walked from the office, she felt Max's gentle hand on her lower back, ushering her down the hall. She also felt Jordan's stare like two lasers boring into the back of her head.

Jordan didn't like Max, and that concerned Erica a bit because she respected the man. But she had a feeling his dislike was more about Max's proximity to Erica than about Max himself. And the bottom line was, Max was going to help her find Molly, and right now, that was all that mattered.

Max felt awful. He couldn't get Erica's disappointed look out of his mind.

He'd followed her to the shelter simply to ensure her safety, walking her inside to make sure everything looked normal, in her eyes at least. Now he stood against the wall and watched her interact with person after person, smiling encouragement with each dip of her serving ladle.

He could understand her wanting to help the shelter's children, but the adults all looked shifty and lazy to his experienced eye. And yet he felt convicted for judging. He'd had a rough childhood, but he'd never been homeless. Was he wrong to judge them all against Tracy's killer?

Yes.

He shifted, uncomfortable with the prodding of his heart, his spirit.

He kept his phone close and his weapon closer. And yet he felt compelled to pray. *Lord, I may be wrong here. Help me change my heart.*

The delicious aroma of the food couldn't quite mask the odor of unwashed bodies. Max noticed it didn't seem to bother Erica.

Max's gaze landed on two men at a table in the far corner. They both leaned forward, their conversation quiet. Max's cop instincts hummed. He was willing to let God change his heart, but that didn't mean he wasn't going to be on the alert for trouble.

The one on the left sported a shaggy black beard and a long, dirty, tan overcoat. The one across from him looked a little better. At least he'd found a razor sometime in the past couple of days.

Together they watched Erica.

Max watched them.

When Erica walked over to their table, he straightened and moved closer to hear their conversation.

"Hello, Jed. Anything else I can get you gentlemen?"

They shook their heads and she moved on to the next table, treating the patrons like they were in a high-class restaurant. Her kindness floored him; her compassion for others stirred his heart in a way he couldn't name.

Max looked back at the two men in the corner. They were tracking Erica with their eyes. Finally, the one on the left rose and sauntered from the building. Max watched him go, suspicion crawling all over him. If he'd still been a cop, he would have called for someone in the area to follow him just to allay his concerns.

The other man stood and also slipped out the door. Max relaxed a fraction, then tensed again.

Would they be waiting for her when she left the shelter?

What if she ended up just like Tracy?

He stepped outside and scanned the area. Nothing seemed out of place. Nothing alarming. No men waiting to ambush Erica on her way to her car.

Nothing to worry about.

And yet he did.

He didn't like the way the two men had paid such close attention to her.

He went back inside.

"Well? What do you think?" Erica asked him.

Max shrugged, unable to admit he might have been wrong, especially in light of what he'd just seen. "Everyone seems calm, friendly, glad to have a hot meal to put in their bellies."

She smiled. "They are. For the most part. They may be-grudge the fact they get that meal at the shelter, but they're not going to turn it down."

He paused, then asked, "Who were those two men sitting

in the corner? The one with the beard and the one with the red ball cap?"

She frowned. "I'm not sure who the guy in the red cap was, but that was Jed Barnes with the beard. Why?"

He shrugged. "Just wondering."

Erica nodded in the direction of a young family. "That's Bill and Mary Lawson, and their daughter Claudette. He lost his job eight months ago. She never graduated high school, but was working on her GED when they were foreclosed on. They take turns taking care of Claudette while the other person hunts for a job. They come here to eat, to hear any news of possible job leads and to regroup."

He had to admit the little family looked about as dangerous as Erica herself.

Erica nodded to her left. "And see those two women? They're sisters who were evicted from their apartment when they couldn't pay the bills anymore. They lost their husbands within days of each other. Neither woman has worked a day in their lives because they stayed home with their children. Children who won't have anything to do with them now."

She went on, pointing out different individuals and giving him background. Against his will, he felt himself softening. And he also felt his heart opening up to Erica in a way that felt out of his control.

Erica touched his arm. "Tessa is waving to me. Let me see what she wants and then I'll be ready to leave."

She started to turn and he grabbed her hand. She looked up at him, a question in her eye. "I know we're on opposite sides of the fence as far as Lydia is concerned, but I want you to know that I think you're a very special woman."

A bright flush appeared on Erica's cheeks. "Well…thank you." He smiled at her flustered thanks and released her hand.

As he watched her walk away, he had to resist the urge

to grab her back, wrap his arms around her and keep her from harm.

Erica twisted the tie on the last garbage bag and opened the back door of the shelter's kitchen. She stepped outside to place the bag in the can, and the door slammed shut behind her.

She whirled and grabbed the knob. Locked. "Of course," she muttered. She knocked and waited.

Most of the volunteers had already left, but she and Tessa and a couple of others had stayed to clean up the dining area and the kitchen. She pounded on the door this time. "Hey! Let me in, will you?"

Where was Max?

"Tess?" she called, her voice starting to sound panicked even to her own ears.

Gravel crunched behind her.

She spun and saw nothing but the back alley with the tall fence. The Dumpster loomed to her left.

Her stomach dipped. She was outside, alone. Normally that wouldn't have fazed her. However, with all of the incidents that had happened over the past couple of days, she would have rather had someone with her.

"Is someone there?"

She sucked in a deep breath. She'd just have to walk around to the front of the building. Simple, right?

A figure stepped out from behind the Dumpster. Shoulders hunched, a black beard touching his chest, he shoved a hand into his coat pocket. Erica froze.

The door opened behind her. "Erica?"

She spun. "Max." Relief filled her. She turned back to the man who still stood beside the Dumpster.

"What's going on?" His tight voice was directed at the stranger.

Erica said, "I'm not sure." She stepped forward, feeling

safe now that she had Max at her back. "Jed, you scared me for a minute there."

"Sorry about that."

"Get your hands out of your pockets," Max demanded, shoving Erica behind him.

"Max…"

"Now."

The man complied. He held a small box in his left hand. "I just wanted to give this to Erica."

Her fear beginning to dissipate, Erica stepped around Max. "What is it?"

"A…a gift." He cleared his throat.

Uneasy again, she watched him. An alcoholic and a drug addict, he'd never been physically abusive to Melissa, but the emotional damage he'd done to the woman had been painful to see. "What are you doing out here?"

"I was going to leave, but wanted to catch you alone."

Max kept his protective stance and said, "Erica, why don't you go back on inside and let me take care of Mr. Barnes."

She considered it for all of a split second. "It's all right, Max."

Jed didn't smile. "You told my wife to leave me."

Max stiffened. "Erica…"

"I didn't tell her to leave you, Jed. I told her she needed a break from the stress of your abuse or she was going to have a nervous breakdown." She would never tell someone to leave a spouse. But take a break? Yes.

"Well, she left me."

Erica's heart hurt. "I hate that it came to that."

"I do, too, but…" His shoulders slumped.

"But?"

"It was the best thing she could have done. The only thing."

Erica relaxed a fraction. Max's defensive posture slackened slightly. "What do you mean?"

"I mean, it forced me to take a good hard look at myself, and I didn't like what I saw so I got help. I've been clean for six months. Melissa said she'd go to counseling with me."

Relief and gladness filled her. "Oh, Jed, I'm so glad."

"Me, too."

Max released a breath and she felt his tension ease. Jed held out the gift to Erica, setting the small box on her palm. "This was my grandmother's. I want you to have it."

"What? Oh, no, I can't—"

"Please. I've been coming in here just about every day for the past three months. After I got out of rehab, I'd look for a job and come here to eat and sleep and work on getting my life in order." He shuffled his feet and ducked his head. When he looked up, tears were in his eyes. "You encouraged me that I could change. That I could be the man that Melissa and my kids needed. I never had anyone do that for me before." He nodded. "I started to believe you after a while. This is just a small way to say thanks. And maybe when you look at it you'll remember that some of us do want help. We just don't know where to get it until someone like you comes along."

"Jed, I...I don't know what to say."

"Don't have to say anything." He gave a half smile. "I'll be seein' you." He turned and walked down the alley to disappear around the corner.

Erica shook her head and silently thanked God for the way He worked.

"What is it?" Max asked. He settled his hands on her shoulders and she breathed in his spicy scent. A scent that was becoming as familiar as her own. One she liked. A lot.

She lifted the top of the box to find a tiny cross pin nestled on the velvet fabric. "Oh, it's beautiful." She drew in another deep breath. "Goodness, I can't keep this."

"I think you have to." She looked up to see him staring toward the end of the alley. "I think he needed to give that to you. It was like he was doing something his grandmother would approve of, and that was important to him."

Erica closed the box and slipped the treasure into her pocket. "This is one of the reasons I do what I do, Max."

"Yeah." The cryptic look on his face didn't tell her anything about what he was thinking. He stared at her for so long, she shifted under his hands. "What is it?"

His eyes grew tender. "Like I said before, you're incredibly special, Erica." He lifted a hand to her cheek.

Her heart thumped at his words, at the feel of his touch, at the look in his eyes.

"I—"

"What about Lydia?" she interrupted, turning away.

He sighed. "Lydia. Right." He hadn't forgotten about her, but he couldn't deny that a part of him wanted to move forward with a relationship with Erica, regardless of their different opinions about Lydia. "I know it looks bad for her, and I don't want to believe she's guilty, but I've come to the conclusion that whatever she's done, she's done. And if she hasn't done anything, that will come out, too. Whatever the result, I don't want it to keep us apart."

Erica's eyes widened in shock. "But—"

Before she could finish, he leaned over and pressed a kiss to her lips. A sweet, gentle kiss that sparked a flame inside her. Her heart and her mind battled it out while she wrapped her arms around him and kissed him back.

After what seemed like forever, he lifted his head, eyes glittering. "I care about you, Erica."

"I know," she whispered. "I care about you, too."

"After we find Lydia—"

She pressed her fingers to his lips. "Don't say anything. Don't make promises. Let's just find her."

Disappointment flashed in his eyes, but he nodded. His jaw looked tight, as though he wanted to say something more, but he held the words back. Finally, instead of saying what was in his eyes, he said, "Come on, let's go talk to Kenneth Harper and see what he knows about Lydia."

ELEVEN

Max couldn't help feeling relieved as the homeless shelter disappeared from view. He had mixed emotions. The people he'd met weren't like the ones he'd arrested as a cop. At least not all of them. Most of the residents were, if not exactly peaceful, at least calm.

Granted, there'd been a few moments with Jed that had stressed him out, but once again, he was reminded not to judge a person by his appearance. He would pray for Jed and his wife, Melissa.

Max glanced at Erica. She had her phone pressed to her ear. "Denise, this is Erica. Peter told me you were back in town. Give me a call and let's catch up. I'll try to get to the hospital to see your father soon. Call me, hon." She hung up with a frown. "I wish she would have called me when she got in town."

"She's probably busy with her father."

"I know, but still…" She sighed. "Denise has been so good about keeping in touch since she left. We've talked on the phone almost every week since she moved."

"I'm sure she'll return your call soon."

"I suppose I could just go up to the hospital."

"Do you want me to drop you off?"

"No, I want to be there for Denise if she wants me to, but right now Molly comes first."

As they drove to the construction site, his mind whirled with other questions he wanted answers to. Starting with Jordan. And if he and Erica were going to have any sort of romantic relationship, Max needed to know those answers. If she would tell him.

"Jordan's not a very friendly guy, is he?"

She shot him a sideways glance he caught from the corner of his eye. "Jordan's all right. He's just hard to get to know."

"He makes it hard."

"I suppose he does."

She wasn't going to say anything about the man, negative or otherwise. Max appreciated her tact but at the same time found it frustrating. He looked at her. "Did you two date?"

"No." A smile curved her lips. He turned his attention back to the road, but all he wanted to do was watch her. He decided he could spend hours just watching her.

"So…is there a history there? A story?" He knew he was pushing but he couldn't seem to stop himself.

At first she didn't answer. About a mile later, she finally said, "Jordan is a unique person. He has a history, but I'm not part of it. All I know is he and Brandon were roommates and best friends in college. About a year ago, Jordan showed up and needed a place to crash. Brandon then talked him into joining Finding the Lost shortly thereafter." She looked at Max and added, "He's very good at what he does."

Max pulled into Brown and Jennings Construction and parked. He didn't really want to hear any more about Jordan. And he didn't enjoy the admiration in Erica's voice when she talked about him.

Jealousy was a new emotion for Max. He seemed to be feeling it a lot lately, and he didn't like it. He opened his door. "Let's go see what we can find out."

Erica nodded, and he chose to ignore the somewhat amused look on her face.

At the desk, Max flashed his private investigator credentials and the young receptionist's eyes widened. "What do you need?"

"To speak with Kenneth Harper."

She got on the phone. When she hung up, she said, "Go through that door to the left. He's waiting for you."

Max appreciated the fact that Erica was allowing him to take the lead on this. As she walked from the car to the office, he could feel her impatience ramping up again. No one else would probably notice, but having spent most of the past thirty-six hours in her presence, he'd learned to read her pretty well.

Kenneth was a short round man with a bald head and blue eyes that flitted between Max and Erica. "Have a seat. What can I do for you?"

"I found your business card in my sister's belongings," Max said. "I wondered what she wanted from you."

Kenneth scratched his head. "We had advertised at some of the local restaurants that we were looking to hire a receptionist. She came in for an interview."

Max sat still, trying to process the information. "An interview?"

"Yeah, but she was just too young and inexperienced. She was up front and honest about the fact that she'd been through rehab, but you can see this place—it's crazy. I needed someone with experience. There just wasn't time to train anyone." He looked at Erica. "You look like the type who would know how to run an office. Want to apply?" The flirty tone in his voice grated on Max.

"How did she react when you turned her down?" Max asked.

Still looking at Erica, Ken said, "She said she understood,

but I could tell she was disappointed. I felt kind of bad about it. Then I saw her name on the news."

"Did you call the cops and let them know she'd been here?" Erica asked.

He flushed and rubbed his chin. "No."

Max lifted a brow. "Why not?"

Finally, the man's eyes met his. "You're not a cop, right?"

"Not anymore."

Ken shrugged. "I didn't have the time to mess with them coming out and asking a bunch of questions I don't have the answers for. Simple as that. If I thought I could have helped them, I would have called, but she was in and out, and I have no idea where she was going once she walked out my door."

"Did you notice how she got here for her interview?"

Ken pursed his lips. "Came in a little white car. Someone else was driving. I remember because the car was blocking one of my trucks and I had to wave it out of the way."

"Male or female driver?"

"Couldn't tell." Another shrug. "Didn't look."

"And when was this?"

"About two weeks ago."

"You got security video?"

"Yeah, but it's only good for a week. Then we start over."

Of course.

Max stood. This was getting them nowhere. Erica rose, too, and held out her hand. Ken eagerly took it.

And held on way too long.

Max put a hand on her shoulder and steered her toward the door, forcing the man to release her. "Thanks for your help."

Thanks for nothing.

Kenneth looked disappointed at Max's possessiveness with Erica, and Max felt a dart of satisfaction shoot through him.

Once outside, Erica planted her hands on her hips. "What was that Tarzan routine about?"

He blinked. "He was flirting with you. I thought I'd get you out of there."

She lifted her chin and he braced himself. "I've had men flirt with me before. I can handle it myself, thanks."

What had he done?

His bewilderment must have been stamped on his face because her eyes softened. She dropped her hands from her hips and said, "Just because you kissed me once doesn't give you the right to do this kind of thing."

Kissed her once? He pulled her to him and kissed her thoroughly. He felt her still, held her a bit longer, then set her back from him and said, "Now we've kissed twice. Have I earned that right yet?"

She sputtered and he grinned, enjoying her discomfiture. Finally, she tossed her hands up and shook her head. "I just mean that I can take care of myself in some situations, okay?

"Sure." He paused. "How am I supposed to know the difference between the situations?"

"I'll let you know."

"Right."

Friday morning, Erica woke early and climbed out of bed around five thirty. She'd finally fallen asleep last night out of sheer exhaustion, prayers for Molly's return and Lydia's safety on her lips.

With her bedroom door locked, her gun in the drawer of her end table and Jordan and Max taking shifts playing bodyguard, she'd felt safe.

Safe enough to grab a few hours of much-needed sleep.

After a quick shower and some time with her Bible and her Lord, she dressed and looked out the window to spot Max sitting in his truck, sipping coffee from a thermos top, eyes narrowed and watchful, taking in the area around him. She grabbed her purse and walked out of the house toward him.

When he spotted her, he smiled, yet it didn't reach his eyes, which darted from one end of the street to the other, then back to her. She shivered, the hair on her neck spiking at the danger she sensed could be lurking in the morning shadows. She slipped into the passenger seat. "You can't do this much longer. You're going to wear yourself out."

"I'm a private investigator. I do this all the time."

"Maybe so, but still…"

"It was quiet last night."

She found herself looking at the strong fingers holding the thermos top in a gentle grasp. Just then, her phone rang. It was Denise. Finally calling her back. "Hello?"

"Erica, I'm so sorry it's taken me this long to call you. I guess Peter told you about my dad."

"Yes. Why didn't you let me know you were coming to town? You know I would have been there for you, sat with your father, whatever you needed."

A sigh came over the line. "I know. And I'm sorry. I guess the only-child syndrome kicked in, and I just figured I would handle it myself. And you're busy with your business. I didn't want to impose."

"Impose? Denise. Come on. We're friends."

"I know, I know. Forgive me, please. You're welcome to come help as much as you want." Another quiet sigh. "But truly there's not much to do. The cancer has riddled his body so now we're just waiting for the end. They've upped his morphine, so…"

It was just a matter of time. "I'm so sorry, Denise. What can I do?"

Max shot her a concerned look and she gave a helpless shrug.

"Nothing right now," Denise said, "but I'll let you know if I need something."

"Okay." Erica frowned.

"On a different note, I noticed Peter wasn't looking so great. He's still using?"

"Afraid so."

Denise paused. "Did he ever say anything about Molly?"

Pain seared her. "No. We've discussed this, Denise. I don't think he had anything to do with her disappearance."

"So you say, but after his threats, you have to admit he seemed like the most likely suspect."

"Yes, it seemed so at that time." She left it at that.

"The doctor just walked in. I'd better run."

"Keep me updated."

"Sure," Denise replied, and Erica hung up.

Max looked at her and raised a brow. She shook her head. "Denise has never given up on the idea that Peter was behind Molly's kidnapping." She told him how Peter had come asking for money for a hit and how she'd refused him. "He grabbed me and pushed me into the wall then stole the money out of my purse. It wasn't much and he threatened to get the money one way or another. Molly disappeared about a week later."

He pursed his lips.

"Sounds like she has reason to believe he had something to do with the kidnapping."

"I know. And I'm ashamed to say that I even entertained the thought for a while, but…"

"But?"

"I don't anymore."

"Any proof?"

"Nope. No proof he did it, and no proof he didn't do it. I choose to believe he didn't. Just like you choose to believe Lydia in spite of the evidence against her. So. Are we going to sit here all day or go find some answers?"

He smiled. "I made an appointment to see Red at eleven. She's back at the rehab facility."

"Well, that was easy. I think that's the first thing that's

gone our way since all of this started." He cranked the car and pulled away from the curb.

Erica bit her lip then asked a question that had been bugging her. "Has Lydia ever accused you of wanting to control or run her life?"

"Yes, that was every other sentence for a while when she was talking to me. Why?"

"Peter said something along those lines the other night."

"It's a manipulation tactic. The addict tries to throw the guilt back on the person who cares for him, make that person feel guilty for not 'helping' him enough. And then when your help isn't the kind he wants, you're being controlling."

She grunted. "It's rather effective." She nibbled on a thumbnail. "Did it work on you? When Lydia used it?"

"The first few times. Until I caught on." He smirked. "And the crazy thing was, I had studied that stuff in law enforcement, seen it in the families of addicts when I worked the streets. It wasn't until a buddy of mine pointed it out to me that I saw it with Lydia."

Erica sighed and leaned her head back. "I don't want to control his life. I want him to grow up and live his life. I want him to have the life God created him to have."

"I know." He reached over and took her hand in his. The feel of his warm fingers wrapped around hers chased some of the chill from her bones. "The problem is, he has to want that, too."

"Yeah," she whispered, then fell silent.

She was glad Max didn't let go of her hand until he had to put the car in Park. Having someone to talk to, someone to hold her made all the difference in the world to her. She just prayed that when they finally found Lydia, her budding happiness wouldn't come crashing down.

TWELVE

Red wasn't happy to see them, but Max hoped she'd come around. He and Erica sat across from her on a love seat—the family room had several for visitors. Max had chosen this room for its less-threatening atmosphere.

Staring at Red, he had a feeling not much threatened her. She stared back, measuring, watching.

Erica said, "Thanks for meeting with us."

The girl shrugged. "Got nothing better to do. So what's this about anyway?"

"Lydia Powell," Max said.

Red froze, leaned forward and took another look at Max. Recognition burned across her gaze. She stood. "I got nothing to say to you."

"Wait! Please!" Erica jumped up and raced after Red. She touched her arm and Red spun, but her eyes landed on Max.

"Lydia told me how you called DSS on her and got her taken away from your mother. She told me she never wanted to see you again. So if she's off your radar then good for her." She turned back toward the hall.

Erica blurted, "She's in trouble and you may be the only one who can help."

Red stopped. She turned and this time looked at Erica. "What kind of trouble?"

"You haven't seen the news?"

"No." A frown puckered the skin between her brows. "The news is boring and depressing." Her eyes flicked back and forth between them.

"Lydia's wanted for questioning in a kidnapping," Erica told her.

"Kidnapping!" Red's eyes widened. "She'd never do anything like that."

Satisfaction and relief filled Max at Red's spontaneous outburst. "I know. But the cops don't. That's why I need to find her."

Erica's lips went tight and he could see she didn't agree with him. Or Red. Renewed sadness hit him that Erica truly believed Lydia had something to do with Molly's disappearance. He'd just have to keep working to prove her wrong.

"She doesn't want you to find her," Red snapped.

"Look, Red," Erica intervened. "Lydia may have some answers we desperately need to find this missing child. But it appears that someone doesn't want Lydia found."

Just like with Bea, they told the story of Lydia being attacked at the crack house. And like Bea, concern filled Red's eyes. As painful as it was for Max to think about his sister's difficult journey, it was good for him to know that she'd met people who cared for her, and worried about her. Just like he did.

"I don't know where she is. I saw her about a week ago and she was acting a little weird. I just thought she was back on the dope."

"But she wasn't?"

"I don't know. It would have surprised me because she was so determined to stay clean. She talked about getting a job and proving to you that she isn't the loser you think she is."

Max winced. "I don't think she's a loser."

Red ignored him. "Now that I know all this, she could have been jittery 'cuz she was scared."

Max's phone rang and he grabbed it to shut it off. Then he saw the number. "Excuse me a second." He stepped from the room, leaving Erica and Red staring after him. "Chris, have you found her?"

"No, but we've got a good idea where she was about four o'clock this morning."

"Where?"

"At Erica's office."

"Please, Red," Erica pleaded, trying to keep one eye on Max, "if there's anything else you know, tell me now."

"I'll think about it." The attitude had returned along with the curled lip, and Erica knew she was done here. Erica thought the young woman might know more than she was sharing, but figured she wanted to talk to Lydia before she told too much.

Max waved her over urgently. Erica said goodbye to Red, and told her to call them if she thought of anything. The look on the woman's face made it clear that that probably wasn't going to happen.

In the car, she asked Max, "Can we monitor her calls?"

"I've already thought of that." He waved his phone at her. "Katie's working on getting a court order and I've got her counselor stalling on letting her use the phone until they can get it set up. Katie wants to question Red, but agreed to hold off and see if she makes any phone calls in the next few hours."

"Does she even have that privilege?"

"Yes, she's been good since she's been here."

Erica nodded. "I'd like to go to the hospital to check on Mr. Dougherty."

"Denise's father?"

"Yes."

"So, Tanner is her married name?"

"Denise was married for a brief time, but her husband left her for another woman."

He winced. "When was that?"

"About a year after I was married." She shook her head. "They seemed so happy. I never would have thought he'd do something like that."

"Jerk."

"Definitely. It changed her, of course." Erica sighed. "She cried on my shoulder and I did my best to help her." She bit her lip. "But it was still a terribly hard time. In order to get through it, she focused on her job and ended up pulling away from everyone, including her family—and me. She'd been offered a promotion at one point, but had turned it down because her husband didn't want to move. After he left, there was no reason for her to say no the second time they offered it. And she left. I think it was a huge relief for her. Even though I missed her, I could tell it was the right thing for her."

He shook his head. "It's good you could remain close in spite of the physical distance between you." He took his eyes off the road for a second and studied her. "You look like you could use a bite. Are you hungry?"

"A little," she said, startled that he'd been able to read her needs just by looking at her. It had been a long time since a man other than her brother could do that.

"How about a burger?"

She grimaced. "How about a salad?"

With a grin, he found a drive-through that served a variety of palates and ordered the food.

"We can eat at my office if you want."

"Sounds good."

Five minutes later, he turned left into the office parking lot. "So you think you'll get together with Denise?"

She nodded. "Of course." She gave a small shrug. "Everything fell apart around the same time three years ago. Molly disappeared, then three weeks later, Denise had to leave. She hated it, but had put off going when Molly was kidnapped. She couldn't wait any longer and I had to encourage her to go. She left. My husband didn't seem to care that his daughter was missing…." Her throat wouldn't work. She cleared it. "Let's just say it was a really bad time in my life and I felt all alone."

Max put the car in Park and looked at her, stunned. "Didn't care she was missing? Why not?"

Erica leaned her head back and closed her eyes. Why had she opened that can of worms? She looked at him. "He never wanted her. Not really. Oh, he put on a good show in public, but at home, he basically ignored her. Children didn't fit in with his philosophy of 'life's a party.'"

He blinked. "Why did you marry him?"

She groaned. "I've asked myself that question a million times. We were high school sweethearts. He was handsome and rich and…"

"And?"

She shrugged. "He wanted me. *Me*." She tapped a finger to her chest. "I'd never had anyone chase after me, make me feel like I was a big deal, like I was special, and I fell hard for that—and him."

Max frowned and she could see his mind spinning. "But what about your brothers? And your parents? You come from a good home."

"My parents provided everything we needed and even a few things people consider luxuries. But they were so consumed with working to make ends meet that they didn't really have time for us kids. Mom was a nurse and took any extra shift she could. Dad was a mechanic and practically lived at his shop." She sighed. "They still work like that. It's crazy." She sniffled and rubbed her eyes. "It wasn't a horrible childhood. I just felt…invisible. Andrew noticed me." She gave another shrug. "I will say this for my parents—they love Molly and have dug into their savings to help try and get her back."

He squeezed her hand and said, "Sounds like your childhood wasn't anything to brag about, either."

She shook her head. "I had it easy compared to you, but you're right—it left some scars. And left me open to Andrew James sweet-talking me and making me feel special. And mistaking that for love. I found out what love was when Molly was born."

"What about Andrew's family?"

"Once he left me, I never heard from them again." She shrugged. "I wasn't good enough for him and neither was Molly. They never really had much to do with us."

"Unbelievable."

Rachel waved from the door and Max released her hand. "Come on. Let's see if we get an inkling of why Lydia would show up at your office in the middle of the night."

As she followed Max into the office, Erica found herself surprised at how easy it had been to talk about Andrew to Max. It wasn't just that he was a good listener—although he was that—it also had to do with the fact that she was finally healing from Andrew's betrayal. Finally letting herself open up to another man. She took a deep breath and offered up a silent prayer. *Please Lord, let this be the right thing to do. Letting Max in my heart means being vulnerable to hurt and disappointment—and I just don't know if I'm strong enough for that. If this isn't what I'm supposed to do, let me know. Soon. Please.*

Max stared at the letter left on the front door. He'd used gloves to pull it from the glass.

Taped there by Lydia.

On Erica's computer, the video footage showed Lydia's

face clearly. She wasn't trying to hide. She wanted them to see it was her.

STOP LOOKING FOR ME. LEAVE ME ALONE. I DON'T KNOW ANYTHING ABOUT THAT KID-NAPPING.

"She's scared," Erica whispered. "Look at her face, her eyes."

Erica was right. Lydia's eyes never stopped darting. Her fingers shook as she taped the note to the door.

Max said, "Paranoia is a side effect of the drugs. Could be she thinks someone is after her but no one really is."

"Look at her eyes when she stares at the camera with that pleading look. They're clear, her pupils are normal."

He saw that. "She moved in close. She did that on purpose," he said. "She wanted whoever looked at this video to see she wasn't high."

Erica looked at him. "So if she's innocent, why won't she come in? She knows we're looking for her."

"You saw. She's scared."

"Or, like you pointed out, she's just paranoid because of the drugs."

Max shook his head. "I don't think so."

"Come on, Max, you need to wake up," Erica said, her voice sharp, cutting into him. "She's just like Peter."

Max flinched and stared. "Maybe so, but just like you're not giving up on Peter, I'm not giving up on Lydia."

She snapped her lips shut and closed her eyes. Took a deep breath. "You're right. I'm sorry."

"Apology accepted." He rubbed a hand down his face. "The truth of the matter is, we won't know anything until we find her."

"Then let's hope this video is a step in the right direction."

* * *

While Max took a phone call, Erica called Katie and asked about the note that had been mailed to her, the note that had warned Erica to stop searching.

Katie said, "I was going to call you. There were a few prints on the envelope—yours, Max's and Rachel's—but that's all. Whoever wrote the note and put it in the envelope wore gloves. Traces of latex were found as well as powder that's common to rubber gloves."

"So you're saying that's a dead end."

"Unfortunately."

Erica sighed. "Okay, thanks for checking for me. You did that fast, too. I appreciate it."

"I want to find her, too, Erica."

"I know you do."

For some reason, Katie was very attached to Molly's case. She'd worked tirelessly during the first few days and weeks after Molly's disappearance. And she was crushed when she had to move on to other cases when the trail ran cold. Yet she still worked on the case on her own time. Erica figured there was a story there, but Katie had never shared it. And Erica hadn't asked.

"I've got the court order. We're waiting for Allison Redmond—Red—to make a phone call. When she does, we'll trace it."

"Okay, thanks."

"Oh, and I saw Brandon coming out of the police station a while ago. I gave him a file you'll be interested in."

"Perfect. Talk to you soon."

Erica hung up with Katie just as Max stepped into her office. "Anything on Lydia?" she asked.

"Nothing."

"And Bea's all right?"

"Yes. She said everything has been normal."

Erica frowned. "I'm glad."

"So why the frown?"

"My head is spinning. I'm having a hard time figuring out what to do next."

Brandon rapped on the door. She waved him in and he slapped a file on her desk. Then he nodded to her salad. "You need protein."

"It has chicken, Brandon," Erica said, with a warning in her voice.

He grunted and she saw Max duck his head to hide a smile. She grabbed the file. "Is this the file Katie sent?"

"Yes."

Erica opened it. She studied it for a moment then looked up. "Another missing child."

"Yeah. She's making a referral. Said they were at their wits' end and maybe you would have some luck with it."

Erica sighed. "I don't have the time. I'm consumed with this new lead on Molly."

"Want me to take it?"

"You feel up to it?"

He rolled his eyes and snagged the file back from her. "I feel up to it." He glanced back at her. "What are we doing for Thanksgiving?"

"Our usual, I suppose. Have you talked to Mom or Dad?"

He grimaced. "No. Not lately."

"Everyone can come to my house," she said. "It needs some cheering up."

He nodded and she saw Max watching them, his eyes following their volley. When Brandon left, he stood.

"You're good at what you do." She lifted a brow and Max shrugged. "Brandon and Jordan both respect you. They listen to you."

"You mean underneath the rolling of the eyes and over-protective instincts?"

A small smile played around the corners of his mouth. "Yeah."

She returned the smile. "You're right, they do." She spread her hands. "I'm a delegator. I see past the forest to the individual trees."

"And yet you see the big picture, too."

"Most of the time." She let out a sigh. "And sometimes I can't see anything but a big impenetrable brick wall."

"Finding Molly?"

"Finding Molly."

Silence sat between them for a moment before Rachel stuck her head in the door. "Someone here to see you."

"Who?"

"Me."

Denise Tanner stepped from behind Rachel and gave Erica a wide smile. Joy rushed through her, and she quickly crossed the office to give her friend a tight hug. "Oh, Denise, I'm so glad to see you."

"I hoped you wouldn't mind me stopping by."

"Of course not." She turned to Max and introduced him.

"This is Max Powell. He's a private investigator...and a good friend. He's helping me track down a new lead on Molly."

"A new lead?" Denise leaned forward, eyes intent.

"Yes. Have you seen the news?"

"No. I've been so busy with Dad I haven't had a moment to do anything normal like watch TV or catch up with friends."

Erica told her about the new evidence, and Denise brushed away tears. "Oh goodness, that's the craziest thing ever. I'm praying it pans out. Do the police have anything else at all besides this girl, Lydia?"

"No. That's why we need to find her."

"You'll find her. I have no doubt about that." She turned to Max. "Erica's like Midas, you know. Everything she touches turns to gold. It's a quality I've envied for years." She gave a light laugh.

Erica tilted her head. "Why would you say that?"

Denise shrugged. "It's true. I always wanted to be like you when we were in high school."

Shocked, Erica stared at her friend. "What? You're kidding. But you're super successful."

"I am now, but when we were growing up, I was always in your shadow." She stood. "But I have you to thank for my success. Wanting to be like you made me work extra hard. You were a huge influence in my life."

Denise's words floored her. She gaped. Max laughed. "I think you've managed to make her speechless."

"I've needed to say those words for a long time now." She wiped a tear. "Okay, enough with the mushy stuff. I won't keep you any longer. I just took a break and ran over here to see you."

Erica gave her friend another hug. "I'm so glad you did. Please let me know if I can do anything for you."

"I will." She shrugged. "Right now it's just hurry up and wait. It's sad, but it's his time and I think I've finally accepted that." Denise smiled at Max. "Nice to meet you."

"You, too."

After Denise left, Erica dropped into her chair. "Well. That was interesting."

Max stepped over and sat across from her. "See? You never know whose life you're going to impact. I'm not surprised she had such great things to say. I've come to discover just how wonderful you really are."

She felt the flush climb up her neck, but forced herself to meet his eyes. "I think you're pretty wonderful, too, Max."

He reached across the desk and snagged her fingers. Just

as he opened his mouth, her phone rang. Shooting him an apologetic glance, she checked the number. "It's Katie."

He sat back. "You'd better take it."

Erica snatched the phone. "Hello?"

"Red called a pay phone located at the mall."

Excitement zipped along her spine. "Are you on the way?"

"We are. And we've got the stores pulling video even as we speak. Detective Lee is on Red at the rehab center."

Erica chewed on her lip. "You think you'll get there in time?"

"I don't know. We're trying to be subtle, go in quiet and see if we can spot her."

"Okay, call me as soon as you know something."

"I will."

Erica hung up and looked into Max's expectant face. "They traced the call."

"Then let's go."

Erica stood. "I'm worried if Lydia's been watching the news, she may recognize Katie or Detective Lee. If she sees them, she'll run."

He ran a hand over his face and pinched the bridge of his nose. "If she sees me, she'll run for sure."

Erica hesitated only a second. "Let's chance it."

He nodded and she followed him out the door.

THIRTEEN

The drive to the mall took about ten minutes. Erica shifted on the seat, impatient to be doing something, anything. She was so tired of waiting on someone else to call with news. She wanted to find Lydia herself.

And yet she didn't want to do anything that would send the girl running. But how could she convince Lydia to talk to her if she couldn't even make contact?

Her phone rang and she snatched it. Denise said, "Are you still willing to help?"

"Of course."

"It was so good seeing you. I've missed you."

"I've missed you, too." Her friend paused. Erica asked, "What do you need, Denise?"

"Do you think we could meet for dinner tonight?"

"Sure." Why would Denise hesitate over asking that question? "You want me to come to the hospital?"

"If you don't mind."

Erica could hear the tears in Denise's voice and her heart broke for her friend. She'd been particularly close to her father, and this had to be killing her. "No problem. What time?"

"Five thirty in the cafeteria?"

"I'll be there." She hung up and looked at Max. "Denise wants me to meet her for dinner."

"I'm glad you two will have a chance to catch up a little."

"I am, too. I'm glad she finally asked me to do something, offered a way for me to help her."

"You're a good friend, Erica."

Max parked and they walked into the food court. Erica pushed the phone call with Denise aside as her nerves hummed. Would this be the day she finally found Lydia and learned what happened to Molly?

With her throat tight and her stomach cramped, Erica ignored her anxiety and scanned the crowd as they walked from the car into the food court. People sat at tables and chatted, others stood in the long lines waiting to order. Erica simply wanted to see Lydia's face.

"She used a pay phone over there," Max said after consulting his phone.

"Have they spotted her yet?"

"No."

Erica felt her hopes start to disintegrate. It was too late. There was no way Lydia would still be hanging around the mall.

"Security has her picture," Max said as his eyes probed the area. Erica could feel the tension, the hope, radiating from him.

"We need to find her."

"I know."

Max's phone rang. He listened for a brief second then his eyes caught hers. "That was Chris. They found Peter's car abandoned on the outskirts of town in an old barn. Guy who owns the place found it and called it in."

"Then it probably wasn't Peter driving it. Or shooting at us."

He shrugged. "There's a good possibility it wasn't him. Then again, he could be the one who abandoned the car."

"I really don't think it was."

He gave her a sad smile. "And I really don't think Lydia was involved with the kidnapping. I hope we're both right."

His words hurt, and she grimaced. Just because they'd grown close in this search for his sister and her daughter didn't mean he had to change his mind to her way of thinking. And she'd better remember that if she didn't want to wind up with a broken heart. Lydia came first for him. And that's the way it probably should be. She couldn't help the small self-ish wish that she'd come first for someone.

His phone rang again. He listened, and hung up. "They think they spotted her over near the arcade."

Erica pushed aside her pity party and checked the mall map. She headed in the direction of the arcade, Max following close behind. Security descended and Erica clenched her jaw. "I thought they were going to be subtle."

"I did, too." He didn't look pleased. "Stay with me."

"Wouldn't it be better if we split up?"

He grasped her fingers. "I don't want to take a chance on losing you."

Losing her? A tingle shot through her in spite of the circumstances. She didn't want to lose him, either. But what if Lydia *was* involved? How would he feel about her then? And how would she feel about him?

She pulled away. "Don't be silly. Security's all over this area." She looked around. "Which is why she wouldn't stay here."

Max sucked in a deep breath. Katie broke away from a group of teens and walked toward them. "She was here. As recently as fifteen minutes ago."

Hope leaped. "Then we have a chance of finding her."

Max's eyes narrowed. "Is there a back door to this place?"

Katie nodded. "I've got officers on it."

"She saw security coming toward her and took off." She

nodded toward the officer who stood near the entrance. "He said she acted like she was waiting on someone."

"Red?" Erica asked.

Katie shook her head. "Red can't leave the rehab center. If she does, leaves before she completes the program, her parents take a loss on what they've paid for her to be there."

"Doesn't mean she wouldn't do it," Max muttered.

"True, but I already called and they said Red was in the social room playing a game of chess with her grandfather."

"So if not Red, who?"

Max sighed and shook his head. "I have no idea."

Katie's radio buzzed and she listened. Her eyes snapped to Erica. "Go to the nearest exit and get out."

"Why?"

"We've got a bomb threat."

Erica gasped. Max grabbed her hand. He asked, "Where?"

"The caller didn't say. We're trying to get a trace on where the call came from." She motioned toward the door. "Security will be evacuating the mall immediately."

No sooner had she spoken than the mall intercom came on announcing the building was closing due to a gas leak. "Please leave in an orderly fashion through the nearest exit."

"Gas leak?" Erica asked.

"Saying there was a bomb threat would cause a stampede," Max said. He cast a glance around. "This isn't a coincidence."

"I know." Katie frowned at him. "You were followed."

"Possibly."

They fell in with the moving crowd, and Erica glanced behind her. "We can't leave yet. We have to find her."

"She's not here any longer," Max stated with certainty.

"You don't know that."

"Yeah, I do."

"You can't." Erica stepped to the side, desperation urging her onward. She simply couldn't leave yet. Not yet. She pushed her way through the throng of people to go in the opposite direction.

"Erica!"

Max's frustrated shout made her grimace, but she couldn't leave without searching for the girl who might have answers about Molly.

She didn't believe there was a bomb.

But what if there was? Was she acting irresponsibly?

Max finally caught up with her as she caught a glimpse of Katie searching the arcade area. Erica rushed toward the detective. "Anything?"

Katie spun. "What are you still doing here?"

"There's no bomb, Katie. It's a trick."

"Doesn't matter. You need to get out." Her eyes flashed. "Get her out of here, Max."

He grasped her upper arm. "Come on, Erica."

"But Lydia—"

"We'll find her. Just not like this." Concern hardened into determination.

And Erica realized something. He was just as determined to find Lydia as she was, and he wasn't going to leave her behind. If there was a bomb, she wasn't only risking her life, but his, as well. She couldn't do that. The thought of him being hurt because of her insistence that they stay in the midst of danger nearly smothered her with fear. "Let's go."

She let him pull her back into the crowd heading for the exit.

"Why would someone call in a—" she glanced around at the listening ears nearby "—gas leak?"

He understood her question and shook his head. "I don't know. Unless it was to smoke Lydia out, but the person wouldn't have any idea where she was in the mall or which door she would leave by."

The crowd shoved and pushed toward the exit. Erica

grabbed Max's arm to keep her balance. He steadied her and she was grateful for his support.

"Erica?"

She twisted to see who was calling her.

"What's wrong?" Max asked.

"I thought I heard someone call my name."

Max looked behind her, but she didn't think he'd be able to spot anyone in this mess.

"Erica! Stop!"

This time he heard it. He swiveled his head and looked behind them.

"Do you see anyone?"

"No. Let's get outside and we'll see if we can figure out who's calling you." He turned back, keeping an arm around her shoulders, and she realized he was doing his best to protect her from the smothering press of bodies.

Just a few more feet and they'd be out the door.

A sudden stinging sensation in her lower back had her spinning and losing her balance.

"What is it?" Max asked as he righted her.

"Something stung me."

His eyes narrowed. "What?"

"My back. It hurt. I—" Dizziness hit her, her throat tightened. Awareness and fear struck at the same time. She gasped, "EpiPen."

He caught on fast. "Where?"

"Purse," she managed to squeak out as her airway closed and darkness took over.

Max had known fear in his life, but it was nothing compared to what he felt at the sight of the blue tinge appearing around Erica's lips. She went limp and he caught her. His heart pounded. He had to get her help and fast.

Pushing his way through the crowd, apologizing for shoving and trampling on toes, he made it to the sidewalk, dropped to his knees and laid her down. He grabbed her purse from her shoulder and dumped the contents beside her.

"Sir? You need to move—" The officer stopped. "What's wrong with her?"

"Not sure." He snatched the EpiPen from the concrete. "Call an ambulance."

"Got one standing by. You'll have to get her to it. I can't let them down here with a bomb threat."

Max nodded. "I know." The officer got on the radio while Max uncapped the EpiPen and jabbed Erica in the thigh.

Within seconds, the wheezing eased and a bit of color came back into her cheeks. Her eyes opened, but looked glazed and unfocused. "Erica, hang in there, honey. I've got to get you out of here. EMTs are waiting, okay?"

She gave him no response other than to shut her eyes. He threw the contents of her purse back into the bag. The officer grabbed it while Max picked her up. Sweat rolled down his back in spite of the chilly temperatures as he rushed toward the ambulance waiting a safe distance away.

Heart pounding, legs pumping, Max reached the ambulance as Erica began to stir. "What—?"

"Hold still. You passed out."

"Bees," she mumbled. "Allergic."

The sting she said she'd felt on her back.

He motioned for the EMT to roll her to her side. With gentle fingers, he lifted the edge of her shirt to look at her lower back. "There." He pointed to a red-and-white welt that looked like a bee sting.

The paramedic frowned as they rolled her back into place. "It's November. And cold. Shouldn't be any bees around here."

Max's blood whooshed through his veins. He had a bad feeling about the whole bee-sting emergency.

The EMT placed the oxygen tubing in her nose and

cranked the air. "Let's get her to the hospital. She needs to be monitored for the next few hours."

Max nodded. "I'll ride with her. I need to call her brother, too."

While he watched the paramedic work on Erica, making sure she continued to breathe, Max called Brandon.

The man answered on the third ring. "Hello?" He sounded out of breath.

"This is Max. I'm on the way to the hospital with Erica."

"What happened?" Worry coated Brandon's question.

"A bee sting."

Brandon gave a snort. "In this weather?"

"Yeah. Weird, right? We'll figure it out after we know she's all right."

"I'll meet you there."

Max rubbed a hand down his face and said a prayer for Erica. The ambulance pulled into the Emergency entrance and within minutes Erica had been whisked away behind secure doors. Max filled out as much of the paperwork as he could, but had to admit relief when Brandon burst through the door. Max waved him over.

"How is she? Where is she?"

"Looks like she'll be all right. I was worried there for a few minutes." Worried sick. Scared he'd failed her. Maybe he didn't need to worry about her working with the homeless. Maybe he needed to worry more about her being with him while he was looking for Lydia.

A sigh slipped out as he settled back to wait. And ponder the next step in the investigation. They needed to figure something out and fast. Erica had almost died. Whoever was targeting her was getting more bold. The thought terrified him.

He looked over at Brandon, who sat beside him. Quiet. Lost in his own thoughts.

"How's the gunshot wound?" Max asked.

Brandon shrugged. "It's healing. I turn the wrong way and I pay for it, but other than that…" He paused. "Do you mind if I ask you a question?"

"Shoot…er…go for it."

Brandon gave a wry grin then turned serious again. "What's with you and Erica?"

Max looked toward the door that had swung shut behind her. "I…she's…we're…"

"Friends?"

"Yes." Max jumped on that.

"More than friends?"

"Yes," he admitted more slowly. He looked Brandon in the eye. "I like her. A lot. And—" he rubbed his suddenly sweaty hands down his thighs "—I think I could love her."

Brandon didn't look surprised. "She's easy to love, but she can drive you crazy."

Max smiled. "Yeah."

Brandon let out a slow whistle. "You've got it bad, don't you?"

The door that led to the E.R. opened and a woman in a white lab coat stepped through, saving Max from having to answer that one. "Brandon?"

Brandon jumped to his feet. "That's me."

Max stood more slowly, trying to read the doctor's face. Brandon asked, "How is she?"

The woman hesitated for a moment. "She's going to be fine."

"But…?" Max asked.

The doctor tilted her head, motioning the men to follow her into a small conference room. "I'm Doctor Caroline Watson. Erica had a reaction to what appears to be a bee sting."

"She's been allergic since she was a kid," Brandon said.

Dr. Watson nodded. "Good thing she carried that EpiPen with her or she wouldn't be here with us."

Max's stomach dropped to his toes. Brandon's face paled. The doctor went on. "I have a real concern about this."

"What's that?"

"I've examined the wound site carefully." She shook her head. "I may be wrong, but it looks like she was injected with bee venom. There's a clear needle puncture in the middle of the welt—it's not a sting from a bee itself." Her eyes took in both men. "That means someone did this to her. On purpose."

Brandon exhaled and caught Max's eye. Max felt a little nauseous at hearing his suspicions voiced. Dr. Watson asked, "You might want to find out if she's involved in something she shouldn't be involved in."

That was a given.

"We'll take care of it."

"I'll have to file a police report."

"Of course. We'll talk to them, too." Max swallowed hard.

"We're going to keep her overnight for observation, but she should be all right to go home in the morning."

Brandon said, "I'll get Rachel to come stay with her."

"Not your mother?" Max asked.

Brandon's eyes shuttered. "No."

Max realized he should have kept his mouth shut. "Right."

The doctor's brow lifted but she didn't ask. Instead, she said, "You want to see her?"

"Yes."

The word flew from Max's lips.

He chose to ignore Brandon's amused look and answered his ringing phone.

FOURTEEN

Erica groaned. Her head throbbed and her mouth felt dry as wool. As she gathered her thoughts, memory returned. She'd been stung. By something.

Her memory stopped there.

A knock on the door forced her to drag her eyes open. Darkness greeted her. It was nighttime?

"Erica?"

Brandon.

"Come in." She heard the croak in her voice but couldn't seem to turn up the volume. Brandon pushed the door open and stepped inside. Max followed, and Erica tried to sit up a little. When her muscles simply wouldn't cooperate, she gave up and studied them. Two men she cared for very much.

They both looked drawn and worried. Weary.

Max stepped to the side of her bed and gripped her fingers. Her heart picked up speed to match the pounding in her head. The feel of his hand wrapped around hers gave her comfort. And even felt like a possible lifeline in the midst of everything. He asked, "How are you feeling?"

"Like I've been hit by a truck."

"You've been out for a while."

She tilted her head. "And you've been busy. Did you find Lydia?" Strength returned at the thought.

"No. But Katie called. She watched the mall video and got a pretty good shot of someone working their way through the crowd to get behind you."

She frowned. "Okay. Who?" Brandon and Max exchanged a look. "Who?" she demanded.

"Peter," Max finally said.

"Peter?" she whispered. "But why?" She remembered thinking someone had called her name. "He was there?"

"Yes. Clear as a bell, and it was obvious he was trying to get close to you. As soon as he did, that's when you cried out and said something stung you." Max sighed. "I was so busy trying to get you out the door and keep you from getting trampled, I didn't see him."

"But he's on the video."

"Yes."

"What about Lydia?"

Brandon nodded. "We watched the video of the arcade room. She was definitely there and it looked like she was waiting for someone." He ran a hand over his eyes. "And Peter was there, too."

Max squeezed her fingers. "Erica, someone definitely injected you with bee venom."

She swallowed hard, grateful she could. The sensation of her throat closing up was one of the worst she'd ever experienced. "Then that means whoever did this is someone who knows me pretty well and knows that I'm allergic to bees."

"Which means it could be Peter."

"No." She shook her head. "He wouldn't do that. He has no reason to kill me." Another exchanged look between the men grated on her nerves. Brandon looked torn, not wanting to believe it, either, but he was a black-and-white personality. He'd seen the video, and she knew he wasn't convinced Peter was innocent. "Where *is* Peter?"

"We don't know. We're looking for him."

"Seems like we're looking for everyone without much success," she muttered.

No one argued with her.

The knock on the door made her jump. Max took a defensive stance and Brandon moved to open it.

It took Erica a moment to process whom she was seeing. "Mom?" she gasped.

Brandon stood with his mouth open.

Shelby Ann Hayes stood five feet five inches tall. She had her auburn curls pulled away from her face with two clips. Erica thought she spotted some gray at the temples.

The woman smiled and approached the bed. "Saw your name on the chart and thought I'd come see how you were doing."

Erica tried to remember the last time she'd seen her mother. At least a year, maybe longer. "What are you doing here?" She blurted the words, then wanted to recall them.

Shelby stopped, her confident expression fading to uncertainty. "Like I said, I just wanted to see how you were doing."

Max stepped to the side like he might slip out the door. Erica grabbed his hand. For some reason, she wanted—no, needed—his support. Brandon still gaped like he couldn't find enough oxygen. Then his mouth snapped shut and his face reddened. "Since when do you care?"

Her mother sighed and said softly, "I care, Brandon. So does your father. We did the best we could."

And Erica thought maybe they had. Her parents had just been too young to have kids. At sixteen Shelby Hayes should have been a cheerleader, not a mother.

"It's a little late," Brandon growled.

"No. It's not," Erica countered. She met her mother's eyes, suddenly sick of the distance, the roller-coaster emotions associated with her parents. And Erica had been the one who pulled away after Molly went missing—she couldn't blame her parents for that.

Her mother had offered an olive branch of sorts. Erica decided to take it. "I'm doing all right. I'll probably go home tomorrow."

"Do you need anything?"

"No. But thanks."

Her mother looked uncertain, nervous and agitated. She kept shooting glances at Brandon, then at Max. Erica introduced him while Brandon glared.

"Well." Shelby backed toward the door, which Brandon didn't waste any time opening. "I guess I'll check on you later. Or in the morning...or sometime."

"Sure, Mom. You do that." The woman turned to leave and Erica called, "Wait!" Her mother looked back over her shoulder and Erica shifted forward on the bed. "Do you know where Peter is?"

Shelby's shoulders slumped in defeat. "No. I've tried to call him several times over the past couple of months. He hasn't called me back."

"If you hear from him, will you call me?"

"I'll call."

Erica felt the shock set in after her mother had left the room. Brandon stepped toward her. "Why are you being nice to her?"

She stared at him. "I'm tired of being mad at her."

"Mad? You should hate her."

Erica looked at Max. "For what, Brandon? Working all the time to support us? At least she was never on drugs, we had warm beds to sleep in and she occasionally hugged us." She swallowed hard. "She wasn't a great mother, and Dad wouldn't win any Father of the Year awards, but they were kids when they had us. They didn't want children, Brandon, but they didn't give us up or separate us or abuse us."

His jaw never softened. "Maybe we would have been better off if they had. Given us up, I mean."

"I refuse to dwell on it. The past is the past."

He stared at her, suspicious and curious. "This seems awfully sudden."

Erica picked at the blanket. "They were crazy about Molly. You saw that yourself. At Christmas they overspent. They treated her like they never treated us. I don't understand it, but maybe it's because they're finally grown up and want to make amends."

"You do what you want. I don't want them back in my life."

"Let go of the anger, Brandon. It won't do you any good."

He grunted. "I'm going to get a cup of coffee." He strode out the door without looking back.

End of discussion.

Erica shook her head then looked at Max. "I need to call Denise and tell her I'm not going to be able to meet her at five thirty."

"Yeah." He shoved his hands in his pockets. "What was all that about letting the past be the past?"

She sighed and leaned her head back against the pillow. "I'm just tired of being angry with them. Sometimes you just have to let things go."

Max nodded, a pensive look on his face. "Yeah, I guess sometimes you do."

"What is it?"

He shrugged. "At least she cares."

Erica stared at him. Her mother would win Mother of the Year award compared to his. "She does, and it's time for Brandon and me—and Peter—to understand and forgive." If Peter wasn't the one trying to kill her. Pain shot through her at the thought, but almost instantly, she realized she didn't believe it. "I want to talk to Peter."

"I know."

"I don't believe he would try to hurt me."

"I know that, too." He leaned over and placed a soft kiss on her lips. "You're an amazing woman."

Erica placed a hand on the back of his neck and pulled him in for another kiss. Then she smiled at him. "You're pretty amazing yourself."

Max cleared his throat and stepped toward the door. "I'd better let you get some rest."

"I'm not sleepy." She yawned and he laughed.

"Right. I won't be gone long."

Erica nodded and closed her eyes. Maybe she would just rest her eyes for a bit.

Just a short nap while she felt safe and the person who wanted her dead couldn't get to her.

Max watched Erica sleep, his emotions in turmoil. Someone had tried to kill her. Just like someone had killed Tracy. His heart shuddered at the memory, and his fingers curled into fists.

But the person after Erica wasn't someone she'd worked with at the homeless shelter.

This was worse.

This was someone she knew.

But who?

He didn't know her well enough to mentally make a list of people close to her who would know about her allergy.

But he thought it odd her mother would decide to pay her a visit. It was such an out-of-the-blue thing. And yet, maybe not. After all, the woman worked at the hospital and she really did care about her children.

And then there was Peter.

A light rap on the door caught his attention. He rose to open it and found Denise Tanner. She frowned, as if surprised to find him in Erica's room. "I got your message. Is Erica okay?"

"She's all right, but she's sleeping right now." Max stepped out into the hall and shut the door behind him.

Denise twisted her fingers together. "My dad's taken a turn for the worse, but I wanted to run up and check on Erica."

"It could have been a lot worse. But she'll make a full recovery."

Denise placed a hand over her heart. "Oh, thank goodness."

"I'll tell her you came by. And I'm sorry about your father, Denise."

She nodded. "Thanks. I'm going back down to be with him, but please call me if you need anything."

Max thanked her and she left.

He went back to Erica. He'd stay with her until Rachel arrived to spend the night. After the doctor had filed her report with the police, and Max had spoken with Chris, an officer was posted at Erica's door. She would have protection tonight.

Her auburn curls lay spread around her, looking like they could set the pillow on fire at any moment. Long, pale lashes lay against her cheeks. She looked peaceful. Untroubled.

He ran a finger down her arm. *Please keep her safe, Lord. My heart's in too deep. If something happens to her, I don't think I'll recover.*

Max vowed to stick as close to her as possible and catch the person responsible for the chaos that had become their lives.

No matter who it was.

The next morning Max beat Brandon to the hospital and into Erica's room by mere seconds. He flashed his ID to the officer standing outside her room, glad to see he was still on duty. As he knocked and pushed open the door, Brandon rounded the corner.

He held the door for the man then stepped in at Erica's welcome. She sat on the bed looking much better than the night before. In fact, she looked great. Alive. Whole. Healthy.

Beautiful.

He wanted to grab her into his arms and never let her go.

She looked up and gave him a wan smile as he stepped in. Rachel sat in the chair frowning. "I'm trying to talk Erica into going home," Rachel said. "But she wants to work her shift at the homeless shelter."

Max felt his heart hit his toes. Holding on to Erica might not be an option. Not if she insisted on continuing her work with the homeless.

Maybe that was selfish, but how could he forget the past and move on? Tracy had gone to work at the shelter that evening, just like she did every Thursday night. Max had been working and when she didn't call to let him know she was home, he'd wondered, but had been knee-deep in a drunk driving accident and hadn't had time to call her until two hours later.

She hadn't answered. Chris Jiles had been called to the scene of her murder then had been the one to break the news to Max.

The investigation had found that Tracy's murderer had followed her from the shelter. He was one of the regulars. He'd also been in need of a fix. At the trial, he'd wept. He hadn't meant to kill her, but she'd fought him when he'd tried to rob her. He'd pushed her down and she'd cracked her head on the sidewalk. She'd died from a broken neck.

Every time Erica walked out the door, he'd wonder if she'd be back. He couldn't live like that. And it wasn't that he still thought every person at the shelter was a criminal or a murderer. It was just his memories of Tracy and how she didn't make it home, memories that still haunted him. It seemed the closer he got to Erica, the more he thought about what had happened to Tracy, and how he was sure he could never go through something like that again.

He tried to hide his reaction to Rachel's announcement. "Why don't you get some rest first? If you collapse at the shelter you won't be doing anyone any good." He paused. "And besides, who's to say your attacker doesn't know your schedule? He could be waiting at the shelter."

"Or he could be down in the lobby waiting for me to walk out the front door. I have no doubt he knows I'm here."

"You have an officer on this room," Max argued, feeling his protective instincts kicking in. "When you leave here, you won't have police protection."

She bit her lip and her forehead creased. Her cousin nodded. "He's right, Erica. You need to stay safe and stay away from the shelter until you find out who's behind all this."

This time Erica scowled. "You don't like me working there, either."

Rachel sighed and shrugged. "Just think about it."

"I have." She rubbed her face and looked at Rachel. "Will you call and tell them I'm not coming?"

"Sure." Rachel pulled her cell phone from her pocket and excused herself from the room.

Max couldn't deny the rush of relief he felt at her sensible response. But what about the next time? What about after her attacker was caught and she didn't have to worry so much about her safety?

Brandon spoke for the first time since entering the room. "I think not going to the shelter is a wise decision. You need to go home and rest, Erica."

"But there's so much to do. Lydia's still missing. And Peter. And Molly." Tears welled in her eyes and Max had to hold himself back from taking her in his arms right there. Instead, he reached for her hand.

Squeezing her fingers, he said, "The cops are looking for

Peter. They'll find him. And we'll find Lydia. I've got calls in all over the place and friends are looking for her. She can't stay hidden forever."

"It feels like she can," Erica said.

From the door, Rachel said, "I forgot."

Erica looked at her. "Forgot what?"

"Peter called, looking for you yesterday. I told him you were heading for the mall. That's how he knew how to find you."

"Did he say what he wanted?"

"No. And I didn't ask." She cast her eyes toward the floor then back up. "I figured he just wanted money."

Erica swallowed hard, and Max wanted nothing more than to take her in his arms and hold her. But since he couldn't do that, he did the one thing he could.

"Come on and I'll take you home."

Brandon lifted a brow. "Well, since I'm not needed as a taxi, I'll check all of Peter's known drug connections."

"And you'll let me know as soon as you know something?" Erica asked.

"Of course."

She sighed. "Then all right. I'll go home."

Max saw her frustration, felt her impatience. After Brandon left, he sat on the edge of the bed and took her hand in his once again. "Everyone is fighting hard to make sure you stay safe."

Her eyes softened and she nodded. "I know and I appreciate it."

He leaned in and placed his forehead against hers. "I don't want anything to happen to you."

Erica met his gaze then shifted so she could give him a light kiss. Max raised a hand to cup her chin and deepened the kiss, needing to tell Erica how he felt about her without words. Then he pulled back and gathered her close.

He relished the moment with her in his arms. But he couldn't help but wonder how long she would stay home before thoughts of Molly sent her searching once again—and right into the arms of danger.

FIFTEEN

Erica woke in her own bed with a start. Heart pounding, she listened. Footsteps, the hardwood creaking, a drawer closing. Anger surged.

Peter.

How had he gotten past the officer sitting outside watching her house? Max had dropped her off so he could continue searching for Lydia. And Peter.

Only it looked like Peter had come to find her before Max could find him.

Erica snagged her weapon from her bedside table and shoved it in the back of her sweatpants. She had no intention of shooting her brother, but if he was high, there was no telling what kind of trouble he'd be.

Maybe the gun would be enough to scare him.

On silent, bare feet, she padded down the hall toward the noise, ignoring the slight dizziness and residual weakness she felt.

At the entrance to the den, she paused. Listened.

And heard voices.

Her rushing adrenaline slowed, but her pulse skittered as she recognized the first voice. Max.

Then Brandon and Jordan.

Erica leaned against the wall and closed her eyes as her blood pressure returned to normal.

It wasn't Peter.

She took a deep breath and ran a hand through her curls. Then did it again and again until she felt presentable. Max didn't need to see her with the rat's-nest, just-rolled-out-of-bed look. Then she felt heat invade her cheeks and wondered why she cared.

But she knew exactly why. There was no denying it.

In spite of their conflicting interests in finding his sister and his issues with the homeless shelter, she had feelings for Max Powell. And she wanted to look nice. She turned and walked back down the hall to her room where she changed into a pair of denim capris and a green shirt she knew brought out the color of her eyes.

With one final look in the mirror and an eye roll at her vanity, she headed back to the den.

Max sat on one end of the couch and Jordan on the other. Brandon sat in the recliner. He looked up when she walked in. "You decided to join us?"

"Didn't know there was anyone to join."

"You were snoring pretty good in there," Brandon teased.

She resisted the urge to revert to her childhood habit of sticking her tongue out and simply rolled her eyes at him. "What's with the good-morning welcoming committee?"

"Wanted to make sure you were safe," Jordan said.

"So all three of you had to come over?" She crossed her arms. "What gives?"

Max quirked a smile at her. "We got a lead on Lydia."

Erica dropped her arms. "Then what are we waiting for? Let's go get her."

"Bea called and said Lydia got in touch with her and is going to come by her house," Max said.

"When?"

"In a couple of hours."

"So what's the plan?"

"We just finished setting that up," Jordan said and stood. "I'm going to Bea's house. I'll let you know when I have Lydia."

Jordan walked right out of the room without another word as Erica gaped. "Wait a minute. What's going on?" She looked at Max. "Aren't we going?"

He shook his head. "You and I are being watched. Brandon, Jordan and I discussed this and we think it's best if the two of them grab her. I don't want to take a chance on leading anyone to Bea's house."

"And you don't think someone will follow Jordan?"

Brandon stood. "That's where I come in. I'm going to make sure he's not followed."

Erica swallowed. "And you'll call the minute you have her?"

"Of course."

She nodded. "All right. I don't like it, but I have to admit it might work. She won't be looking for you guys."

"Exactly." Brandon leaned over and kissed her forehead. "Take care."

"You be careful. You're still healing from one gunshot wound—you don't need another."

He grinned at her and flexed his arm. "Good as new." But she caught the slight grimace before he turned his back.

"I mean it, Brandon."

"I know you do." He looked at Max. "Keep her safe."

Max nodded and Brandon left.

Erica slumped onto the couch next to Max. "I hate this waiting. It reminds me so much of the first few weeks after Molly disappeared."

He wrapped an arm around her shoulders and leaned in

to place a kiss on the top of her head. "I know. But hopefully this time it's going to pay off."

"I miss her so much," she whispered. "Even after three years, I miss her with an ache that feels like it'll never heal."

Max pulled her close so that she could rest her cheek against his chest. He smelled good. Woodsy and spicy all at the same time. She appreciated his attempt to comfort her. She looked up to find him gazing at her. Their noses touched and she drew in a deep breath. Then his lips were on hers. She reveled in the softness, the comfort he was trying to express. When he lifted his head, she wanted to pull him back. Instead she sighed and snuggled against him.

His hand stroked her hair and they sat in silence for several minutes. Then he said, "I noticed your Bible on the end table by the recliner."

"Mmm-hmm."

"Is that how you've stayed strong through everything?"

"Yes." She picked at a piece of nonexistent lint on his shirt. "I don't understand why God allowed Molly to be kidnapped. At first I thought maybe it was because I wasn't a good enough mother, that I was doing something wrong and that He was punishing me by taking her away from me."

His arms tightened. "I'm sorry."

"I kept reading the Bible, trying to find out how I could make things right. How I could make God love me again so that He would send Molly back to me." She felt a tear slide across her nose. She sniffed.

"What did you find?"

"I found that God didn't take Molly away because I'd done something wrong or been a bad mother." She raked a hand through her hair. "And I learned that if God loved me enough to send His son to the cross before I was even born, then He loved me unconditionally."

"How long did it take you to discover that?"

"It took about a year for me to believe it. Especially after Andrew walked out."

"What finally convinced you?"

She smiled against his chest then pulled back to look into his eyes. "One of the most well-known verses in the Bible. John 3:16."

"'For God so loved the world that He gave His only Son…'"

"'…that whoever believes in Him will never die, but have everlasting life,'" she finished. "It hit me that He died for me before I was even born. For me. Molly's disappearance didn't take God by surprise. Could He have stopped it? Yes. But He didn't and I have to admit, that hurts. I don't always understand his ways, but I choose to believe Him when He says He has a plan for everyone. And that includes Molly."

"What if she's…"

"Dead?"

"Yeah."

Erica heaved a sigh. "I know it's possible. It's possible she died the day she disappeared." She swallowed past the lump in her throat. "I'm not out of touch with reality. I know the statistics when it comes to missing children. So…if she's dead, then I'll have to figure out how to move on. Somehow, I'll have to let God be my strength, because I'm not strong enough to do it on my own." The last sentence was a mere whisper. She wasn't even sure she'd said it aloud.

He pressed a kiss to the top of her head and said, "I want to be here for you, too, Erica."

Longing gripped her. "I want that, too, Max." She leaned back from his embrace, immediately missing his warmth. "But let's see what happens with Lydia before we go any further."

"I don't know that I want to do that."

She stared at him. "Well, I think we have to. We have no

idea how this is all going to turn out, and I don't want to put you in the position of having to choose between Lydia and me."

Max pulled her back against him while he thought about what Erica had said. Even as he held her, he wondered what he'd do if it came down to making that choice.

He couldn't abandon Lydia. He wouldn't give up on her.

And he couldn't give up this woman who had so filled his heart in such a short time that he was almost willing to call his feelings for her *love*.

Which scared him, for a whole bunch of reasons.

Lord, I'm going to need Your help.

"I don't think it's going to come to that," he finally said.

She gave him a sad smile. "Let's hope not."

Her phone rang and she pulled it from her pocket. She listened for a moment then sat straight up. "You did? When?" Her eyes locked onto his. "I'll be right there."

"What?"

"Someone saw Lydia eating breakfast at the shelter."

Max felt his gut twist. He knew what her next move was going to be. He reached for his keys even as she stood and shoved her feet into the shoes she'd kicked off.

She looked at him. "You're not going to try and talk me out of going?"

"Nope."

"Good decision."

"I figured." He opened the door and followed her out as he called Brandon's number. "I'll drive."

She didn't argue.

Max drove them to the shelter with a familiar tightness in his belly. He hated that place and all it represented. He'd avoided it for the past four years, refusing to drive past it if at all possible. Now in the span of two days he was making yet another visit.

He'd lost his mind.

Or fallen really hard.

Or both.

Ten minutes later, he pulled into the parking lot and told his racing heart to slow down. Erica was out of the truck and bolting for the door.

"Erica, wait!"

She paused for a slight second, her impatience clear. He caught up fast and they entered together. The smells hit him again. Just like before, a mixture of fried chicken, pine cleaner, unwashed bodies and air freshener.

But he also noted the atmosphere of calm once again. It wasn't a cheerful, homey place, but it wasn't a cold institution, either. Patrons sat at picnic tables in a large cafeteria, eating and chatting.

He processed the information as his eyes scanned the area, desperately searching.

And not seeing the one person he wanted to see.

"Where is she?" Erica asked. He didn't answer. Instead, he pulled out Lydia's picture and began going table to table, asking people if they'd seen her.

He saw Erica make a beeline toward the rotund black woman in the pink warm-up suit. Tess, if he remembered correctly.

The two hugged, and Max went back to showing Lydia's picture. Finally, a young woman with a toddler in her lap said, "I saw her a few minutes ago." She looked around. "She was sitting by herself and looked real sad."

Hope leaped inside him. "Did you see where she went?"

"She left when you walked in." The woman pointed. "Went right out the back."

Max bolted for the back door.

"Max?"

Erica's questioning voice stopped him for a fraction of a second. "She went out the back a few minutes ago."

Erica left her friend's side and followed him.

* * *

They pushed through the back door of the kitchen and Erica glanced around, disappointment washing over her. "She managed to disappear again."

"But she's around here somewhere."

Erica stood still as half an idea came to her. "We need to stop chasing her."

"What?" Max spun toward her, disbelief on his face.

She shook her head. "We need to give her a reason to come to us."

Max appeared to think that over. "Okay. How do you propose we do that?"

"I haven't worked out all the details, but…what if we…" She paused. "No, it'll have to be just you."

"What?"

"What if you go on the news and make a plea for her to come home?"

"What if she doesn't see it? And to be honest, she probably wouldn't care if she did."

Erica chewed on her bottom lip. "I feel sure she's watching the news every chance she gets." She pursed her lips. "When you're one of the top stories, you can't help yourself. And I bet Lydia will care more than you think about seeing you making such a public plea."

He swiped a hand down his face. "I suppose it's worth a try." He pulled out his phone. "Let me make some calls."

Erica's phone vibrated. "Hello?"

After a pause, Erica heard, "Hi, it's Denise."

"Denise? Are you okay?"

"He's gone." Sorrow thickened her friend's voice. "His pain is over. All the arrangements have been made. I'm going home now. I just need to…think. Be alone."

"I'll come over right now." Lydia was gone, Max was working on the plan and Denise needed her.

"No. It's okay. Really."

"I'll be there soon."

She hung up and felt Max watching her. "You take care of getting on the news. I'm going to be with Denise for a few hours."

"You can't be alone, Erica."

She sighed and closed her eyes. "Brandon and Jordan are at Bea's house."

"I'll take you to Denise's. I can make these calls while I wait on you."

"You're sure?"

"I'm sure."

Erica wanted to weep. They'd missed Lydia by a few minutes. She couldn't believe it. Hopelessness tore at her, but she refused to give in to the feeling. They had a plan, a plan that might actually work.

God, I don't know why this is happening, but I sure wish You'd at least let me talk to the girl.

She rode in silence as she pondered what Max should say on his plea on the news, but her frustration was making it hard to think clearly. Visiting with Denise would be good for her—she would focus her energy on her heartbroken friend, instead of constantly thinking about herself and her situation. She prayed she could offer Denise some real comfort.

Max pulled up to the house. She started to get out and he placed a hand on her arm. "Hold on a second."

"What is it?"

"I just want to watch and listen for a few minutes."

Puzzled, she stared at him as she settled back into the seat. "Okay."

For the next five minutes, he kept the window down and watched the street. Finally, he said, "All right. You can go. I don't see anything that rings my alarm."

Of course. He was worried they'd been followed. "I won't

stay too long. She said she wanted to be alone, but—" she shrugged "—I want to check on her."

"It's fine." He held up his phone. "I have plenty to keep me occupied. And I'll be watching the house."

"Okay. Thanks, Max."

He leaned over and planted a quick kiss on her lips. She felt a real, genuine smile on her face and realized it had been a while since she'd actually grinned. "What was that for?"

"You're growing on me."

She reached up and touched his face. "The feeling's mutual."

"Good, because I learned something today."

"What's that?"

"I've been petty and judgmental since Tracy's death." He swallowed hard. "Being at that homeless shelter was very hard at first…then as I began talking to people, I started to see them as individuals, not as a group." He sighed. "They're not all bad people."

"No. They're not." She paused. "Some fit into that 'bad' category, but the majority are there through no fault of their own. Most of them just want a bed to sleep in, food to eat and the opportunity to make their lives better."

He nodded. "I saw a little bit of that yesterday. And even more today." He reached up and put his hand on hers. "You made me see that. And I've been praying for God to change my heart." He smiled. "I think He's answering that prayer."

"I'm glad, Max. I'm so sorry about Tracy. It was a horrible experience, I'm sure. But don't let it keep you from giving people a chance."

"Yeah." He nodded toward the porch where Denise stood. She must have just noticed them and stepped outside. "She's waiting on you."

Erica turned to see Denise, hands on her hips, shoulders stooped with weariness. She asked Max, "Are you coming in?"

"Maybe in a little bit. I'm going to make those calls and check in with Brandon and Jordan. Go be with your friend."

"Okay. Thanks."

She got out of the car and walked toward Denise.

"You didn't have to come, Erica." Tear tracks stained Denise's cheeks, and her mascara had smudged under her eyes.

Erica wrapped her arms around Denise's stiff form. "Of course I did." Why was Denise so resistant to her?

Denise finally offered her a pat on the back and said, "I'm cleaning out Dad's house. You sure you want to tackle that?"

"If you're feeling up to it and ready for the bombardment of memories, I'll be glad to help."

"I'm not ready, but I have to get it done and get home."

"Then let me help you."

Denise dropped her arms, seeming to lose the will to fight Erica's insistence. "Okay, I appreciate it."

Erica followed Denise into the house and noted the boxes everywhere. "You don't want to move back here, Denise?"

"No. Never. I'm quite happy where I am. As soon as Dad's buried, I'm going home."

Erica didn't realize until that moment that she deeply missed her friend and had been hoping she'd return, but she supposed she understood. Denise had made a life for herself in a new place with a great job—and probably good friends. She wouldn't be selfish and wish otherwise. "Where do you want me to start?"

A sigh slipped from Denise's lips. "I don't care. Everything has to go. The house goes on the market next week."

Erica blinked. "My. You've been busy."

Denise shrugged. "I didn't have anything else to do while I was sitting in the hospital waiting for him to take his last breath. I figured it was better to be productive rather than to be in denial."

Erica was a little taken aback, but that was Denise. Blunt and to the point. "All right, why don't I tackle the kitchen?"

Denise stared at her a moment, then her face crumpled. "I already miss him," she gasped. "I can't believe he's gone."

Erica moved to take her friend in her arms. "I know," she whispered against her hair. "It'll be all right."

"No, it won't. It really won't." She blinked and reached up, grasping her hair with her hands in despair. "I killed him."

Erica was stunned. "Of course you didn't kill him. Why would you say that?"

Denise let out a harsh sound that was half chuckle, half sob. "I'm sorry. I'm not making any sense."

"What do you mean you killed him?"

Denise pulled away and swiped her eyes. "He's never forgiven me for leaving. My choice to leave was something he couldn't get over, and now he's gone."

"But you always talked about how you enjoyed his visits. He flew out there a couple of times a year to see you. If he hadn't forgiven you, he wouldn't have bothered." She rubbed her friend's arm.

Denise shook her head. "Never mind. I'm just…"

"Grieving," Erica finished for her. "Come on, let's get busy. Maybe some physical activity will help."

Denise's grief-stricken face returned to normal. "Yes, of course, you're right. I was working in his bedroom. I figure if I can get through that, I can make it through the rest of the house."

"Do you want me to do that for you?"

"No. I need to. You finish the kitchen. It's almost done anyway."

Erica picked up one of the boxes leaning against the wall and a roll of packing tape. "All right, the kitchen it is."

"The bubble wrap is on the table."

"Got it."

Erica moved into the kitchen and taped the box together. Several boxes already sat stacked next to the back door. It wouldn't take much to finish. Just the pantry and the few dishes stacked on the counter.

For the next thirty minutes, Erica worked quietly, thinking. As she packed, she realized a startling fact.

No one was here for Denise. Her father had just died and no one had come by. She couldn't remember if the man had been a member of a church or not. She thought so, but maybe not.

Erica frowned as she pulled the tape across the top of the last box. Where were Denise's other friends and family? She tried to think of other family in the area.

An uncle. A cousin or two she remembered from childhood but hadn't kept up with so had no idea if they still lived in town or not. "Strange," she muttered. Then shrugged. She was glad she'd come to support her friend. Perhaps Denise hadn't kept in touch with anyone when she'd left. But that didn't explain why no one else was mourning her father.

Finished with the kitchen, Erica walked to the window and looked out.

Max still sat in his truck, the phone pressed to his ear. A lump rose in her throat. "Please, Lord," she whispered. "Let us find Lydia and Molly. Show us where to look next. And keep them both safe."

The prayer echoed in her mind, filling her heart. But she just couldn't quell the uneasy feeling that time was running out.

For everyone.

SIXTEEN

The more Max thought about it, the more he felt they were missing something. Something that was as plain as the nose on his face, only he couldn't see it. Mentally, he ran down a list of everyone in Erica's life that he could think of. Unfortunately, he didn't know whom he might be missing. But those he did know…

Who would know she was allergic to bees?

And who would even have access to the venom? Anyone doing an online search, probably.

Peter was the obvious suspect. But Max didn't like the obvious. Everything that had happened with Peter could have been set up. From stealing his car to luring him to the mall.

And then there was Rachel. She had some jealousy over Erica and Denise's friendship, but was it a motive to kidnap her own niece? And if so, where had she kept the child all this time? Assuming Molly was still alive. If Rachel was the kidnapper, the cold knot in his belly told him Molly was dead.

Please let her be alive, God.

He pulled the file on Molly from under his seat and opened it. One thing kept nagging at him. One of the witnesses said she saw a woman that looked like she could be with the group but wasn't. He read the witness's statement. "I only noticed her because she seemed so alone. Lonely. I felt sorry for her. The next time I turned around, she was gone and I really didn't think anything more about her until Molly disappeared and you started asking me questions."

Katie had questioned the woman further, but had gotten only a brief description. Curly red hair pulled up in a pony-tail, large sunglasses, thin, kept her hands in her coat pocket. The police had written her off as a visitor because no one re-ported seeing Molly leave with her.

The more Max thought about it, the more he was convinced the woman had something to do with the kidnapping.

He pulled out the sketch the artist had created based on the witness's description. Unfortunately, it wasn't a very good one.

"Curly red hair," he muttered. Rachel? An idea hit him. He grabbed his phone and called Brandon.

"Any luck with Lydia?" he asked when Brandon answered.

"No. Just sitting here watching the house, drinking coffee and trying to figure out who could be after Erica."

"I have an idea and I need your help."

"What do you need?"

He glanced at the window he'd seen Erica looking out of a few minutes ago. "I need you to get me into Erica's house."

"Why don't you just ask Erica?" Max was glad Bran-don seemed curious, rather than suspicious. Maybe the man trusted him.

"Denise's father died."

"Oh. I'm sorry to hear that."

"Erica's over here at Denise's father's house. She's help-ing her pack it up. I don't want to bother her until I figure out if I'm right or not."

"Right about what?"

"I'll explain when I see you. I'm going to call Chris and see if he can take over for me."

"This can't wait?"

"No."

Chris arrived within fifteen minutes, pulling up behind Max's truck in his squad car. Max got out and shook hands with the man. "Nothing's going to happen to Erica while I'm watching out for her."

"If she sees you out here and asks what's going on, just tell her I'm following up on a lead and I'll be back soon, all right?"

"Of course."

Max climbed back in his truck and took off for Erica's house. Within minutes, Max was in her drive. Brandon pulled up behind him. "What's this bright idea?"

"I need pictures of everyone in Erica's life at the time of the kidnapping."

Brandon blinked. "That's a lot of people."

"Okay, not everyone, but anyone who was especially close to her."

"She's got an album inside that has tons of pictures from the time Molly was born to the time she disappeared. Erica never looks at it anymore, but I know where it is. Come on."

Brandon turned the alarm off and led the way inside. Max waited for the man to get the album. Brandon handed it to him. "What are you going to do with it?"

"Show it to someone. Come on."

Erica was halfway through the china cabinet in the dining room when Denise walked in. "You're making good progress." Surprise tinted her voice.

"Well, it's a no-brainer kind of job." Denise had pulled her dark hair into a ponytail. The dark circles under her eyes tugged at Erica's heartstrings. "I'm sorry you're going through all of this."

Denise shrugged. "It's the way it is. It's not fair, but whatever."

"I owe you an apology," Erica said.

Denise's brow rose. "Whatever for?"

"For not being there when Todd left you."

Her friend's jaw tightened. "That was a pretty bad time in my life."

"I know." Erica dropped her head. "I was so consumed with my own marriage and Molly that I wasn't there for you like I should have been."

Denise sighed. "I don't know that it would have helped if you had been. You couldn't have done anything." She shook her head. "I wasn't exactly there for you when Andrew walked out."

"You let me cry on your shoulder many times in the three weeks before you had to leave."

Denise grabbed her hand. "I just want you to know that was one of the hardest things I've ever done in my life."

Erica gave her a soft smile. "I understood." She drew in a deep breath. "So…should I finish up the china cabinet?"

"Sure. I'm going to see what I can do about that bathroom in the hall upstairs."

Erica turned back and within minutes finished packing up the cabinet. She took another box and the tape and went down the hall to the guest bedroom and stepped inside.

She could hear Denise upstairs on the phone once again as she set the box on the floor. Denise's belongings lay strewn around the room. Erica was turning to leave, figuring Denise would want to take care of this room herself, when her eye landed on a photo album on the bedside end table.

Curious, she picked it up and sat on the bed.

She'd wondered about Denise's life ever since the woman had moved to New Mexico. In their weekly conversations, Denise had talked about her job, the friends she'd made and the fact that she didn't miss anything about her hometown except her best friend.

Erica opened the album and stared down at her daughter's face.

* * *

Max found the witness from the zoo at a church potluck dinner in the gym, also known as the Family Life Center. It had taken them only about thirty minutes to track the woman down, and then Brandon had returned to join Jordan at the stakeout at Bea's house.

Max stood at the door and scanned the crowd.

A woman in her late fifties stepped away from the food line. "You look exactly like you described yourself."

He smiled, anxiety tightening his gut. If his suspicions were correct, Erica would be devastated.

"Mrs. White?"

"Yes."

"I appreciate your being willing to do this."

"It's not a problem. That day has haunted me." She pressed a hand to her lips. "They never found the little girl, did they?"

"No, ma'am."

They found a couple of chairs and Max handed her the photo album. Mrs. White settled in and opened it in her lap. "I remember watching the news, praying they'd find her. Eventually, the news stopped running the story." She looked up. "They ran something the other day about it, didn't they?"

"Yes, ma'am."

She nodded and went back to the album, flipping pages all the way to the end. Max's heart stopped when she didn't point to anyone. It had been a long shot, but he'd hoped…

"Nothing?"

She shook her head but didn't hand the album back to him. Instead, she closed her eyes. "The woman I saw that day was all alone. She looked lonely and kind of sad. I never really saw her face, but I remember her specifically because of her coat."

"Her coat?"

She nodded and opened the album to one of the pages in the beginning. "I have one almost just like it. It seemed like every time I turned around that day, I was seeing this woman in my coat."

"Why would you have seen her so much? You weren't with the day care."

"I was with another school. We were all following the same guide around the zoo."

"What about the man that was spotted?" He pointed to a picture of Peter. "Did you ever see him there?"

She shook her head. "I didn't notice him." She pointed to a photo. "This looks like the coat the woman was wearing that day. In fact, I'm pretty sure it's the same one."

She turned the album around and showed him the photo. She was pointing to a picture of Denise.

"But you said the woman had curly red hair. This one has brown hair."

"She did. But that coat and those sunglasses look identical to the ones I saw. The only thing different is the hair color." She tapped the picture. "This is her, I know it."

"A wig," he whispered. "She wore a wig." So it wasn't Rachel, the cousin she trusted. But the person's identity and subsequent betrayal would still be devastating to Erica.

A cold ball of fear centered itself in the pit of his stomach. He thanked the woman and called Erica's number as he rushed to his car. Her phone rang four times, then went to voice mail. He hung up and tried again. Same thing.

His phone rang, distracting him for a moment. He ignored it, slipped behind the wheel and called Chris. As soon as the man came on the line, he said, "Denise kidnapped Molly. Get Erica out of there. Play it cool if you can—don't tip Denise off. I've got backup on the way coming in silent."

As soon as he hung up with Chris, his phone rang. He pulled out of the church parking lot even as he answered.

"We've got Lydia," Brandon said. "She's scared out of her

wits. I've called Rachel to come stay with us, hoping a female presence will calm her down."

"Good idea." He should have thought of that. He filled Brandon in on where he was headed and why. "The witness picked her out of the photo album, Brandon."

"Denise!" The shout made his ears ring.

"I've got law enforcement on the way there now. Chris is going to get her out of the house, hopefully with no problem."

"That's not good."

"Tell me about it."

"I'll be there as soon as Rachel gets here. Jordan can handle this."

An idea hit him. "Let me talk to Lydia." He turned left, then right. Almost there.

"She refuses to take the phone."

Anger infused Max. "Put her on speakerphone. She has to hear this."

"Go."

"Listen to me, Lydia. I don't know if you had anything to do with this kidnapping or not, but a woman is in danger because of the person who took Molly. I need your cooperation, not your silence. Hate me if you want, but help me save Molly's mother."

A sob sounded.

"Lydia? Talk to me. Help us. If you don't, you could find yourself in jail, and I don't think I could handle seeing my baby sister in that awful place."

"Oh, Max. I'm sorry." She was crying.

And in that horrible moment, Max had to face the facts: his sister *had* had something to do with Molly's disappearance. But what? What had been her role?

He forced his emotions away. He'd deal with them later. Right now, he had to do everything he possibly could to get Erica away from Denise.

"Get yourself together and help me. I need to know whatever you can tell me about Denise's state of mind."

"At first, she was so nice. I thought she was helping me. I thought I was helping her. But then I saw that the little girl I was babysitting was really Molly James. I was going to take her back to her mother, but then they left town and Denise said she'd kill me if I said anything."

She was crying so hard now it was difficult to understand her. "The men with you are going to bring you to me, okay? I may need you."

"No! I'll tell you everything, but you gotta just let me leave, okay?"

"Let's see how it all plays out, Lydia."

He couldn't just let her leave, but he wasn't going to tell her that. Not now.

"Max, she tried to kill me twice already."

"Yeah," Max hardened his jaw. "There's been a lot of that going around."

"I thought if I could just disappear, she'd leave me alone. Then they put my face on television and everyone started looking for me."

"You should have come in, honey."

"I couldn't! Even in jail, she could get to me. I'm just so tired." Sobs broke through, and Max heard Brandon come back on the line.

"We'll be there shortly."

"I'm going to check back in with Chris and make sure he's got her out of there."

He hung up and dialed Chris's number once again as he did his best to beat the cops to Denise's father's house.

Erica wasn't sure how long she sat there and stared at that photo.

Shock bombarded her. Molly was alive.

Her blood pounded in her veins as her heart beat so hard she thought it might explode. She flipped the pages. Pictures of Molly. From infancy to now, at the age of six.

How did Denise have this? Why?

Her hands shook. She started at the beginning of the album again, staring at the first picture. It was Molly as an infant, a photo Erica had taken and given to Denise.

She flipped to the last picture. Molly—older, but Molly all the same.

Her baby.

In this photo album on Denise's nightstand.

She felt frozen. Disconnected from reality.

And then time sped up. She had to call Katie. And Max.

Max. He was right outside, still patiently waiting for her to come out. She snapped the album shut and replaced it on the nightstand as her brain scrambled to put everything together. She stood and turned to find Denise in the doorway.

"What are you doing in here?"

Erica's blood hummed as she bit back the desire to scream at her former friend and demand to know where Molly was. Instead, she took a deep breath. She couldn't blow this, couldn't let Molly slip through her fingers once again.

"I…I thought I'd see what else I could pack up for you. I didn't realize this was the room you'd been using." She picked up the box and the tape. "I was just going to check out the den area. Make sure you got everything."

Denise nodded and smiled. "I have to return a couple of phone calls. Don't worry about this room…it's mostly my stuff. Why don't you help me with the garage?"

"Sure," Erica managed, nearly choking on the word. "I can do that."

Denise turned and left.

Erica swallowed hard. How long had Denise been standing there? Had she seen her looking at the album? Her phone was in her purse on the kitchen table, and Max was outside. She would be fine. She tried not to dwell on the fact that Denise— her best friend—had tried to kill her. Several times.

The betrayal cut deeper than Erica could have ever imagined. This woman had stolen her child and tried to kill her. Anger churned with the fear as she moved toward the bedroom door.

She had one goal: getting her daughter back. All she had to do was get out of the house safely without tipping Denise off that she knew what the woman had done.

On shaky legs she stepped out of the bedroom. The hall stretched before her, empty.

Where was Denise? She said she had to make some phone calls, yet Erica didn't hear her talking. Her stomach twisted itself into knots, perspiration dotting her brow. *I'm coming, Molly. I'm coming.*

Erica listened, trying to pinpoint where Denise might be. But she still heard nothing. Had she already gone into the garage to make her phone calls while she packed?

Or was she waiting for Erica so she could ambush her?

Nausea swirled, her heart pounded.

No. Stay calm. Denise didn't know she'd seen the pictures.

Or did she? She'd been in the doorway when Erica put the album back on the end table. How long had she been standing there?

Erica had to get out of the house. She couldn't confront Denise, not this way, not all alone with no one realizing she was in the house with a killer.

A knock sounded on the front door.

Erica made a beeline for it.

As she passed the living room, a blur moved to her right, pain lanced up the back of her head and down her neck and then blackness reached out to snatch her.

SEVENTEEN

Max pulled up to the curb two doors down from the house and parked. He hopped out of the vehicle and saw Chris on the front porch standing to the side and knocking on the door. Foreboding set in. He shouldn't still be knocking. What was taking so long?

"Chris?"

The man turned, his eyes flashing. "I can't get either of them to come to the door. Denise told me to hang on, but that was the last thing I heard."

Max followed Chris's example and stood to the side of the door. He raised his knuckles and rapped. "Erica?"

No answer.

Chris growled, "We need backup."

"It's on the way. This neighborhood is off the beaten path—it's going to take them a bit to get here. I got here fast because I was just a few miles away." He knocked again. "Erica? Denise?"

"Just a minute! I'm in the middle of a phone call."

He heard the impatience in Denise's voice. Why wouldn't Erica answer him? What was taking so long? Why wouldn't Denise open the door?

He realized he needed the answer to those questions. And now.

"She has no reason to suspect we know anything, right?" Chris asked quietly.

Max thought for a second. "No. But what if she has reason to suspect that Erica knows something?"

He looked at Chris, whose narrowed eyes and tense jaw said he wasn't happy about that possibility. Chris asked, "You want to knock it down?"

Max hesitated. He hadn't heard anything from the inside that caused him concern—other than Erica's lack of response.

"Might be better to ask for forgiveness rather than permission in this case. If she does suspect something by the time backup arrives, things could get ugly." He glanced at the still-empty road. "Will you check and see what their ETA is? I'm going to see if there's an unlocked door or window I can slip in."

Chris nodded and pulled his phone from his pocket as he leaned forward slightly and peered through the window. He jerked back with a grim frown. "She's got a gun."

"What?" Max's mouth went dry with fear for Erica.

"I just caught a glimpse of it." He shifted to look in again. "I can't see anything else. Just her back now."

"Where's Erica?"

"I can't see her."

Max felt his heart start to thud double time. Erica was in danger. Again. "Then we don't want to kick the door in—yet. Denise doesn't know we know anything. I'll try one more time—try to keep her talking until backup gets here."

Prayers on his lips, he lifted his fist and knocked.

Erica groaned. Why did her head feel like it was going to explode? She tried to open her eyes, but it seemed like lead weights pressed down on them.

The pounding continued.

"Go away!" A shrill voice cut into Erica's brain. She winced at the pain.

"Let me in! I need to talk to Erica!"

Max?

"She's in the bathroom!"

Erica tried to block the pounding and shouting. With her eyes closed, she concentrated on keeping her stomach settled.

"Wake up, Erica," the voice hissed.

Fear shot through her, but she couldn't figure out why.

Nausea swirled harder.

The pounding on the door continued.

Something nudged her side. She ignored it. A sharp jab in her ribs made her gasp, and she opened her eyes. Debilitating pain sliced through her brain, and she gagged.

"A headache, huh?"

Denise. Her best friend. Her confidante. Her shoulder to cry on.

Her…daughter's kidnapper.

"Denise…why?"

"I need you awake. I've got some guy pounding on the door asking about you. That man, Max, I think. I need you to tell him everything's all right and get him to leave."

Erica's eyes finally focused. They landed on the weapon in the woman's left hand. "Why didn't you just kill me?"

She'd almost prefer it to the pain in her head.

"Are you not listening? Get him out of here then go in the garage and get in the car. We're leaving. Now get up."

With a gasp and a groan, Erica forced herself to roll to her side. She got on all fours and pushed herself up. Dizziness hit her; nausea won out.

Erica raced to the kitchen trash can and lost what little food she had in her stomach. She sank to the floor and held her head in her hands, praying for relief.

"Denise, I need to talk to Erica." Max sounded firm and in control. Calm and detached.

"Hold on, she's coming!"

Erica took a deep breath and watched the woman from the corner of her eye.

Denise wasn't quite as calm and in control as she wanted Erica to believe. Her hands shook, her eyes darted and Erica knew she was thinking, trying to work out a plan that would allow her to escape. She also knew that if Max wasn't outside pounding on the door, she'd be dead.

And Denise would be gone.

If Denise managed to disappear, Erica would never find Molly. She shut her eyes and prayed while Denise paced and Max continued to insist on talking to her.

"Get over there and get rid of him." Her eyes were cold. "Or I'll make sure you never see your little girl again."

"Hold on, Max! I'm coming." Erica managed to say the words above a normal volume, but she paid for it with another wave of nausea. Bending over, she closed her eyes and waited for it to pass as she wondered if he'd heard her.

The pounding on the door stopped. Her head was another matter.

She made her way to the door. "Max, there's…um…so much stuff blocking the door. You'll…um…have to just hang on a second while we move it."

"Then let me in the back door."

"Too much stuff there, too. Just…give us a minute." She met Denise's eyes. Satisfaction gleamed there.

Erica's legs gave out and she sank to the floor once again. She dropped her head and cradled it in her hands while she spun scenarios. "Can you at least get me a bag of ice for my head?"

"No," Denise hissed. "Into the garage and in the car. You drive."

"Denise, I'm seeing double. I can't drive."

Erica felt Denise move in front of her. She cracked her eyes and saw feet. She looked up. Denise's upraised fist, curled around the gun, made her flinch. "Get up," the woman ordered.

"I can't." She licked her lips. "And if you hit me again, I'll be down for the count."

Denise pointed the gun in Erica's face. "Then I'll kill you now."

Erica knew if she got up, she'd black out again. And who knew what Denise would do at that point. "I thought you needed me," she said.

Denise's frustration was evident on her face. "I do." She walked to the window and looked out. "I can't believe this. This wasn't supposed to happen. Just one more day and I would have been gone." She turned back. "Only now if you don't answer the door, they're going to know something's wrong."

"I'm pretty sure they already know." So why weren't they knocking the door down? "Where's Molly?"

"I don't know. She was kidnapped, remember?"

Erica's fingers balled into a fist—it was all she could do not to use her last bit of strength to plant it right in the woman's face. That wouldn't help. She had to stay calm and in control if she wanted to see her daughter again.

"You just threatened that if I didn't do what you wanted, I'd never see her again. Don't bother denying that you took her."

"She should have been mine in the first place." Denise opened the door in the kitchen that led to the garage. "Get in the car."

"If you'd get me some ice, it might help. But if I move now, I'll just pass out."

Denise blinked at the change of subject. Erica had done a brief course on hostage negotiation. She'd taken it out of curiosity when she'd become a skip tracer. Now she did her best to remember everything from the class. Unfortunately, she was having trouble focusing. Her vision dimmed.

No, no passing out. Stay awake.

Cold filled her palm. She looked down at the ice pack Denise had fixed for her. Guess she didn't want Erica passing out after all.

Erica placed the ice against the back of her head and winced. It hurt and felt wonderful all at the same time. "You said you killed him. He knew, didn't he?" she whispered.

"What?" Denise stumbled back like Erica had jolted her with a Taser.

"Your father. He knew what you'd done. And the secret killed him."

Bitterness hardened Denise's eyes, and she lowered herself into the chair behind her. "He found out on his first visit. It wasn't like I could hide her. He was horrified." Her lips thinned. "But I convinced him Molly was much better off with me. I told him how her own father didn't want her and how you were too messed up to be a good mother." A slight smile curved her lips. "When Dad saw how wonderful Molly and I were together, he let it go. He fell in love with her just like I did and was the best grandfather ever."

Was she crazy? Erica looked into her eyes and saw no sign of insanity. Just anger that she'd been caught, and a desperation to escape that sent shards of fear slamming through Erica. Desperation was not a good thing for a woman with a gun in her hand.

Gun.

Erica stilled. Her gun was in her purse. Her head still throbbed, but the debilitating nausea had passed. However, Denise didn't need to know that.

The pounding on the front door resumed. "Erica? Come

on. What's taking so long? Are you all right? Open the door. I need to talk to you."

Denise jumped and cursed.

"I'm coming," Erica called, looking at Denise as she stood on wobbling legs. Would Denise really shoot her?

"Hey," Max yelled, "you've got me worried, you two. Open the door or I'm going to kick it in." She heard the fear in his voice.

Denise aimed the gun at the door, and Erica screamed, "Max, she's got a gun!"

The bullet pierced the wooden door and Erica dropped to the floor in case Denise decided to swing the gun around in her direction. Pain throbbed through her, blackness threatened once more and she closed her eyes, fighting desperately to hang on to consciousness.

"Denise!" Max called. "Put the gun down."

"Go away!"

"It's all over. We know you took Molly. The cops are pulling in now."

Denise panicked. "No! No. No. No." She fired the gun again and again into the door, bullets sending wood fragments flying. "Go away! I'll kill her! Go away!"

Erica rolled into the kitchen and under the table to the opposite side.

Max kicked the door down and spun into the foyer as Denise pulled the trigger again. Erica moved from her position under the table and tried to scramble toward Max. "Stay still!" Denise screamed at her. She slammed the end of the barrel against Erica's head, sending another wave of lightning through her brain. A cry escaped her and she sank back to the floor.

Max rolled into the next room, taking refuge behind the wall.

Erica felt sick wondering what she should do, desperate

to figure out how she could help Max help her. If her head would quit pounding, maybe she could think.

"Denise, put the gun down," Max said.

"Move to the other end of the table and sit," Denise ordered Erica, holding her weapon against Erica's temple. Erica swallowed hard as she moved at a slow, deliberate pace. She could see Max's foot in the mirror above the fireplace. She couldn't believe he'd burst through the door like that. He could have been shot.

The phone rang.

Denise jumped. She kept the weapon trained on Erica as she backed up two paces and grabbed the handset. Erica noticed how she held the gun like she knew how to use it, and that she kept Erica between her and Max's line of fire should he come around the corner of the door.

"I want to leave," Denise said into the phone. "I have my car in the garage. We're going to get in it and leave."

Did she really think the police would just let her drive off? That Max wouldn't stop her? "Denise. It's over."

Her former friend stared at her and snapped, "Stay still."

Erica obeyed, cradling her head, acting weaker than she felt. She needed time to build her strength while making Denise think she was still wobbly. She also needed to come up with a plan.

"What are you going to do, Denise?" Max called from the den.

"I'm thinking." She stopped at the window and peered out from the side. "They probably have snipers ready to shoot me the minute they get a clear shot, don't they?"

"Probably," Max said. "That's standard procedure."

"They won't shoot if you surrender," Erica said softly.

"Surrender? Not a chance. My little girl is waiting on me."

Erica swallowed the sob that threatened and bit her lip. She drew in a steadying breath as she inched her fingers toward her purse on the table.

Max sat on the other side of the kitchen wall and prayed. Prayed for Erica's safety and for the wisdom to know what to do with the woman holding Erica hostage. He sent a text to Katie telling her the layout of the house, the situation in the kitchen and the fact that he didn't have a plan but was thinking.

Katie texted him back.

Sit tight. Negotiator coming. For now it's U and me.

Sit tight? Not likely.

He kept his eyes on the mirror that gave him a pretty good view of the kitchen. He could see Denise still had the gun on Erica, but he couldn't see the table where Erica sat.

Erica would be all right. She had to be.

His phone vibrated.

Give me more details on the layout.

The home phone rang until Denise grabbed it and disconnected it. She tossed it on the table almost within reach of Erica.

Then Denise's cell phone started up.

He texted Katie back everything he could see.

Katie wrote, She won't talk to me.

Max called, "Denise. Will you please talk to the detective?"

"No. I won't listen to another word from her. She's just trying to stall me and keep me from getting out of here."

He sent another text to Brandon, asking him to get the police in New Mexico to check on Molly at Denise's residence.

He wouldn't put it past Denise to have Molly moved even as she was involved in a hostage situation.

"Will you at least talk to me?" He wanted her talking, not working on a plan.

"There's nothing to talk about. I need to think so I need you to shut up."

He paused for a moment, praying for the right words. "All I want is for Erica to be safe. I'm not a cop. I'm not a negotiator. And I really don't care if you get away as long as Erica's safe. Will you let me help you? Can we help each other?"

For a moment she didn't answer. He moved slightly to his left, hoping for a better visual, even though it meant putting himself closer to the line of fire.

With the shift, he could see more of the kitchen. And he could see Denise. She held the gun steady on Erica. All he needed was a distraction. If he could get her to move the gun away from Erica even for a split second, he might be able to get a shot.

And it would have to be the best shot he'd ever made.

EIGHTEEN

Erica glanced at the clock as her fingers crept toward her purse. Her first two attempts had been interrupted. But she had to do something. Distract Denise. Get her gun. *Something.* She managed to hang the phone up, but so far it had remained silent. The waiting dragged across her nerves like nails on a chalkboard.

"How does Lydia fit in with all of this?" she asked.

Denise scowled. "That brat. I tried to help her out. I paid her to do something worthwhile, and she betrayed me."

"Betrayed you? How?"

"She figured out who Molly was and was going to go to the police. I could see it in her eyes."

The phone rang, cutting into Erica's confusion.

Denise snatched the handset. "Stop calling me!"

Erica could suddenly hear Katie's voice—Denise must have hit the speaker button. "Denise, we have to talk or we won't be able to resolve this," Katie said. Erica nearly wilted hearing her friend's calm voice.

Denise tensed up, a vein in her forehead jumping. "You either arrange for me to leave here with a live hostage or you get to clean up two dead bodies. Your choice."

A slight pause. "I'll have to talk to my superior about that."

"Then I suggest you start talking. You have thirty minutes.

If you don't give me the answer I want at that time, then it's over." She hung up. Denise screamed, "Get out of my house, Max! Get out!"

"I'm not going anywhere."

"You want me to shoot her? I'll shoot her right here and right now!"

"If you do that, you have no chance of ever seeing Molly again," Max said. "None."

Erica swallowed hard as she watched Denise lose hold of some of her control. She needed her to get it back before she did something even crazier than what she was already doing. "Denise."

The woman looked at her. "What?"

"Why? Just tell me why. What did I do to make you hate me?"

Tears sprang to Denise's eyes, and hope burned in Erica's chest that the woman might still have some feelings of warmth toward her.

"Because you had it all, and I got squat."

Erica's hope dissipated. Confused, she shook her head. "I don't understand. What do you mean I had it all? My parents worked 24/7—you had parents at home who loved you. For me, money was always tight, but you never seemed to lack—"

"At school," Denise hissed as she shook the gun in Erica's face. Erica prayed it wouldn't go off during the rant she could see coming. "You were the popular one, voted most likely to succeed, voted prom queen, had the best grades." She contracted her empty hand into a fist. "I was nothing next to you. The boys didn't notice me, the teachers compared the rest of the students to you and then Andrew asked you out…" She stopped and dropped her head, but the gun never wavered. "It was just too much."

"So you stole my child?" Erica stared at her. The conversation was working. Denise seemed to have forgotten about Max. Erica dared a glance at the door and saw nothing.

The woman's head snapped up. Eyes blazing, she asked, "Do you know why my husband left me?"

Erica blinked at the sudden change in topic. She racked her brain to remember what Denise had said about the man she'd been married to for such a short time and why he'd left. "I guess I assumed it was another woman." She frowned. "But now that I think about it, I don't think you ever said."

"Because it was too shameful. Too…awful." Erica simply looked at her. Denise waved the gun toward the ceiling, then let her hand drop to her side. "I can't have children. That's why he left me."

Erica swallowed hard. She hadn't known that. Even as the reality of what had happened sank in, she was nearly overwhelmed with gratitude. Molly was alive. She'd been with a woman who loved her.

Loved her enough to commit murder for her.

"They know you have her, Denise. It's only a matter of time. The only way this is going to end well is if you let me go." She swallowed hard and forced the next words out. "I'll push for leniency. We'll prove you were in a depression, that you weren't thinking clearly. I won't press charges."

Denise stared at her. "You would do that?"

"Yes," Erica lied. "Yes, I'll do that if you'll just put the gun away. We'll walk out of here together."

"No." Denise shook her head. "You're lying."

"Denise, in all the years you've known me, have I *ever* lied to you? Ever?"

Denise hesitated as she thought. Then she swallowed. "No. I really don't think you have."

"Well, I sure wouldn't start now."

A tear rolled down Denise's cheek. "I thought after a while, you would stop looking for her. That you would get back to a life without her." Denise lifted the gun to Erica's head again. "Why couldn't you just let her go?"

Max felt his heart stop in his chest at the sight of that gun against Erica's head once again.

They were running out of time.

He held his phone out with the camera option on and, although, it was awkward, managed to snap a picture. He pulled it back in and looked at it. He texted the picture to Katie.

Her immediate reply:

Can Denise see front door?

Not at moment. Can u hear?

Yes. We have ears. Erica's doing good. Working on a distraction.

I can give u that.

What do u have in mind?

He answered in four short words.
She responded, Too dangerous.

Only choice. Get ready.

Don't do anything stupid.

He almost smiled. It was too late. In an incredibly short period of time, he'd fallen in love with a woman he could probably never have. But he planned to do his best to convince her she needed him in her life. Because he sure needed her.

That is, if they both got out of this mess alive.

Motion at the front door caught his eye. A uniformed SWAT member nudged the front door open with his foot.

"This is ridiculous." In the mirror, he saw Denise move toward the kitchen door, giving her a perfect view of the front door, too.

He held up a hand to the SWAT member. The man froze.

Max shifted. Now that Denise had moved, he could get a better view of the kitchen. Denise stood next to the garage door. Erica still sat at the table between them. He could get off a shot, but if he hit Denise and her finger pulled the trigger, she wouldn't miss Erica.

He kept his hand up, silently telling the SWAT members to stay back. If Denise saw them, she'd panic.

A scraping sound from the kitchen drew his attention away from the phone.

"What are you doing?" Denise sounded frantic, worried. "Sit down."

"I'm not sitting here anymore." Erica sounded calm. Too calm. "I'm walking out that door and going to get my daughter."

"Sit down!" the woman hissed. "I've already sent a text to the person who has her and he's moving her. You'll never see her. Never!"

Max peered around the corner, his heart pounding out his fear for Erica. What was she doing?

Almost faster than he could blink, Erica grabbed her purse by the strap and swung it at the weapon in Denise's hand as she dropped to the floor.

Max yelled, jerking Denise's attention from Erica. She spun toward him, eyes wide with fury. A crash from behind him made him duck as Denise pulled the trigger. He fired back in her direction.

Two more shots sounded and then there was a brief second of eerie silence before chaos erupted and the SWAT team swarmed in. One of them kicked the weapon away from Denise, who groaned and coughed as she was cuffed.

"Clear the rest of the house," the man ordered.

In a few short minutes it was deemed clear, and EMTs were allowed to enter.

The second he was allowed to move, he flew to Erica's side and helped her out from under the table. Pale and trembling, she leaned against him. "She has Molly. She took my baby."

"I know, but we're going to get her back." Shielding her from the sight of Denise and the paramedics working on her, he tried to lead her from the room.

Erica resisted, pulling away from him. "What is it?" he asked her.

She didn't answer. Instead, she walked over to the woman who'd betrayed her in a way that he couldn't fathom. Denise was conscious, but her breathing was labored. She looked up at Erica and grimaced. She gasped out again, "Why couldn't you just let her go?"

Erica's fingers curled into fists and Max wondered if he'd have to step in to keep her from belting the woman lying bleeding on the floor.

But Erica simply said, "If you thought I could do that, you didn't know me at all."

Erica's head still throbbed but joy bubbled inside her.

Her nightmare was over. She would get her daughter back.

She looked up at Max and linked her fingers with his. This time she let him lead her out into the chilly afternoon.

She shivered and he gave her fingers a squeeze. Just that small gesture conveyed his compassion, his sympathy. She gave him a weary smile, hoping he could see the gratitude she felt all the way down to her soul.

Katie strode up to her. "Are you all right?"

Erica nodded and winced. "I will be if I can remember not to move my head."

"Let's get you checked out." Katie waved several EMTs over.

"I will later. I want to find Molly." She needed to wrap her arms around the little girl, hear her voice. She'd have to take time to get to know her again, and allow Molly to know her. There was so much to do to repair the damage.

"First things first, Erica," said Max. The closest EMT approached her and shone a light into her eyes. She blinked.

"Pupils are even."

She grimaced. "I have a hard head."

"It's still bleeding some. Let me get that cleaned up for you." He reached for a box containing his medical supplies.

"Erica?" She looked up to see Brandon and Jordan standing next to the ambulance. Brandon broke away and raced over to wrap her in a bear hug. "You okay?"

"Yeah," she whispered against his cheek.

He let her go and said, "I've got some great news. Molly's on her way home." He looked up and caught Max's eye. "She lands tomorrow morning at eleven."

Tears flowed from her. This time it was Max who wrapped her in a hug. She clung to him and sobbed. Then she laughed, trying to ignore the pain in her head. "My baby's coming home, Max."

"I know." He gave her a quick kiss that was over much too soon, in her opinion. She caught him before he pulled away and said thank-you by planting his lips back on hers. He chuckled, deepened the kiss and lifted her off the ground.

When he let her go, his smoky eyes said they'd be talking. About everything.

Jordan cleared his throat and Max looked up from the sweetness of Erica's lips, wondering if he was going to have a fight on his hands. But the man's eyes conveyed a resigned sadness. He gave Max a small smile that said more than any words could have.

Max nodded. Message received.

"Max?"

He turned to see Lydia standing next to Rachel, uncertainty in her eyes. She looked fragile, breakable. His heart constricted and he held out his arms. She burst into tears and Max didn't hesitate to transfer his hug from Erica to his baby sister. "It's going to be all right, Lydia."

"No, it's not," she wailed. "It's never going to be all right again."

He could feel Erica beside him as he gripped Lydia's upper arms and pushed her away to stare into her eyes. "Look at me, Lydia." She sniffed. Stringy blond hair hung in her eyes. He pushed it away from her face and tilted her chin up. "It's really going to be okay." He nodded to Katie, who came over. "I need you to take her downtown and Mirandize her."

"What?" Lydia gasped and jerked away from him, eyes accusing and scared.

"This has got to be done right for when this goes to court," he explained. "I need you to look at a lineup of pictures and tell us which one is the woman who paid you to babysit Molly." He wanted a positive identification just for his own peace of mind. The last thing he wanted was for Denise to get off on a technicality—if she survived.

Her attention caught, she stopped crying. "Who?" She drew in a shuddering breath.

"Let's go downtown and let Katie walk you through everything."

Katie took an unhappy Lydia over to her unmarked vehicle and helped her into the backseat. Max turned to Erica. "We'll follow them downtown and see what Lydia says, okay?" Erica nodded.

Once she was bandaged and declared concussion free, she climbed into his truck and they headed for the police station.

Max gripped the wheel, so tense he thought he might snap it in two. "I suppose I owe you an apology."

A sigh slipped from her. "No, you don't."

"Lydia apparently had something to do with the kidnapping, and I wouldn't even—"

"Max, stop." She placed a hand on his. "Let's just see what she has to say, all right?"

Gratitude at her sweet response swelled within him. He shot her a look that he hoped conveyed his feelings and nodded. "All right."

NINETEEN

Erica leaned into Max. Her head hurt, but that didn't bother her nearly as much as her heart. The betrayal and sheer fury she felt toward Denise rocketed through her. Max's arm around her shoulder helped. It felt right.

She'd started to tell him so when they walked into the observation room but she didn't have the chance. Katie's partner, Gregory Lee, entered the room and stood beside Max.

Erica trained her attention on the scene in front of her.

Lydia sat at a table on the other side of the glass. Katie had several photos spread out on the table, and a young woman in her midtwenties stood nearby behind a video camera. "Rolling," she said.

Katie said to Lydia, "I want you to tell me when you see the woman who paid you to watch Molly. The woman who threatened you and stabbed you."

Lydia took a deep breath and nodded. "Okay."

Katie laid the pictures out one by one. When she placed Denise's picture in front of Lydia, her gasping cry was all the answer Erica needed.

"We got the right person," Max said.

"Did you doubt it?"

"No, but better to confirm it than not."

Katie said, "You know her."

Lydia nodded and squeezed her eyes shut. "Yes."

"Two more questions, Lydia."

"What?" Lydia kept her eyes shut.

Katie said, "Open your eyes and look at me."

Lydia did. Tears shimmered on her lashes, and Erica felt Max tense and lean forward. He wanted to rescue his sister. She thought he might get up and rush into the room. Instead, he clasped his hands behind his head and let out a slow breath.

When he dropped his hands, Erica reached over to curl her fingers around his. He shot her a grateful look. Her heart ached at the pain in his eyes, but she was proud of him for realizing Lydia needed to face this on her own. When she came out on the other end, Max would be there for her. But this—she had to do this herself.

Katie asked, "Do you want a lawyer?"

"No, I don't want a lawyer. I don't need one."

"Because it's your right to have one."

Lydia slapped a hand on the table and leaned forward. "I don't want one."

"Fine. Did you help the woman you identified as Molly's kidnapper? Did you help her take Molly that day?"

"No!" The horrified cry burst from Lydia. "I wouldn't do that!"

Katie continued her line of questioning, and Lydia never wavered from her insistence that in the beginning she didn't know what Denise had done.

Max asked, "Gregory, can you get me in there?"

"Why?"

"Because Katie's not asking the right questions."

Gregory studied him for a moment, then said, "What questions do you think need asking?"

"Let me talk to Lydia, Greg."

Gregory nodded. "I'll ask her."

Within minutes, Katie walked into the observation room. Max said, "Let me talk to her."

"Why don't you tell me what to ask her?"

"I'll get more out of her. If she had anything to do with the kidnapping, I'll get her to tell me."

Katie studied him. "I'll have to clear that with my captain."

"Sure."

Erica studied Max. "I'm sorry, Max."

He met her eyes. The grief and defeat she saw there nearly broke her heart. She stepped up to him and wrapped her arms around his middle. His chin dropped to rest on her head. "I really didn't think she'd have anything to do with it."

"I know." She paused. "What are you going to do if she has to do some jail time?"

She heard him swallow and then pull in a deep breath. "I don't know, Erica. I truly don't know."

Erica nodded against his chest. "I'll be there for you if you want me there."

For a moment, Max didn't move, then he gripped her upper arms and set her away from him. At first, Erica thought he was upset with her and pushing her away. But he simply leaned his forehead against hers and said, "Thanks. I'll let you be there—if it comes to that." A short pause. "And even if it doesn't I still want you there."

Erica kissed him lightly and stepped away from him when she heard the door open.

Katie said, "He said you could 'visit' her. The visit will be recorded. Lydia knows this."

"Fine."

Lydia jumped up and rushed to Max as he entered the interrogation room. "Get me out of here. I didn't have anything to do with that kidnapping."

"Then why do you have a thousand dollars hidden in a shoe box in Bea's house?" he countered.

Lydia's eyes went wide. Her lips formed an O but no sound came out. Max nodded. "I found it. I had to convince Bea you were in serious trouble before she'd give me the box."

Lydia's gaze shot to the door as though Denise stood outside ready to pounce. "*She* gave it to me," Lydia whispered. She shuddered. "I was working for her, helping her, I just didn't know I was helping a kidnapper." She gave a humorless laugh. "I was going to quit being such a brat to you. My eighteenth birthday was an eye-opener for me. Believe it or not, rehab taught me a few things about what it means to have family who loves you. I finally saw you cared, that everything you did was out of love." She smiled at his raised brow. "Don't think it was as easy as I just made it sound, but…"

Stunned, Max asked softly, "What happened, Lydia? I don't understand what you're saying."

Lydia sighed and looked at her brother. "I was going to surprise you. Show you I could change, stay clean. Make you proud that I had a job, that someone would trust me with her child…" Her teeth caught her lower lip and she gave a quivering sob, but Max watched her gain control.

"Oh, Lydia…" he sighed. He didn't bother to remind her she could have come to him.

"I promise," Lydia said. "I didn't know she wasn't Denise's daughter. Not then." She turned to the mirror. "Erica's watching, isn't she?"

"Yeah."

To the mirror—to Erica—Lydia said, "Denise told me her husband was trying to take her daughter away from her and she had to keep the little girl hidden. She told me he hit her and their daughter, and that she was leaving him. I wanted to help her. She told me I had to be willing to commit myself to four weeks of almost total hiding. At the end of the four weeks, I could keep the thousand dollars. I agreed. I didn't know anything about the kidnapping. The only television I had was for videos for Molly."

"So you didn't see the news?" Max asked.

"No. Not until almost three weeks after the kidnapping. I ran out to get some more pull-ups for Molly. Instead of going to the grocery store I went to the gas station around the corner. I saw Molly's face on the television and heard how she'd disappeared from her zoo trip and her mother was anxiously waiting for her to come home." Lydia's hands shook as she swiped her hair back from her face and shot another glance at the mirror. "You got up there and pleaded to your daughter's kidnapper to bring her home. You cried and you told Molly how much you missed her. That's when I realized the truth. I ran back to the apartment to grab Molly. I was going to take her home."

"But?" Max asked.

"Denise must have seen something in my face. She grabbed a knife and stabbed me."

He winced. "I thought that stabbing was related to a drug deal gone bad."

Lydia turned back to her brother. "I know. And I let you think that. I couldn't tell what I knew because Denise said she had evidence that would send me to jail. Evidence of drug use, evidence that I'd been the one to kidnap Molly. Everything. I couldn't say a word or I'd go to jail." She swallowed hard. "Who would believe a junkie over a successful businesswoman?"

"And the best friend of the grieving mother," he muttered.

Lydia nodded. Katie stepped inside the room and asked, "How did the clothes show up in the crack house three years later?"

Lydia bit her lip and swiped a hand over her face. "I was so tired of running. Denise kept people after me all the time, warning me to keep quiet, saying that she was watching me. I figured it was only a matter of time before she just had some-one kill me. So—" she shrugged "—I put the clothes and hair bow in a bag and gave them to Red to give to the cops if any-thing happened to me."

"They were found in the crack house."

"I know. I saw that. She probably sold them to another junkie for a few ounces of crack." Her eyes hardened. "Shows you just can't trust people."

Max said, "No, you can't trust the *wrong* people. Some people you can trust."

"Why were you at the mall that afternoon when you ran from us?"

Lydia rubbed her red-rimmed eyes. "Red said Denise called her and told her to tell me that she'd give me enough money to leave town and never come back." She swallowed hard. "After Red called, I set up the meeting where there were a lot of people because I didn't know what she'd try. I was going to take the money and run." Lydia lifted her chin and tears glinted. "I'm sorry, Max, but I was just tired. Be-yond tired."

"I know. I just wish you'd have trusted *me*."

"Well, it was a setup. I caught a glimpse of her gun and ran."

After a few more minutes, Max left Lydia and made his way back to the observation room. He'd done his best to help her. Now they just had to wait to learn if the charges would be dropped or if the D.A. would push to prove Lydia was in-volved intentionally rather than accidentally.

Erica looked worn out. He said, "I think we have the whole story now."

She nodded. "Denise had that bee venom all ready to use on me when she had the chance, didn't she?"

"Looks that way."

"And I told her exactly where I'd be. All she had to do was head over to the mall and call in a bomb threat, lose herself in the crowd and…" She blew out a sigh. "Well, I set myself up with that one, huh?"

"You didn't know."

She grimaced.

A knock sounded, and he turned to see Brandon and Jordan at the door. Brandon said, "Sorry to interrupt, but we've got some news. We've found Peter." Max lifted a brow, his silent question clear. Brandon said, "He's alive. Barely. They've taken him to the hospital."

"What happened?" Erica whispered.

"Looks like a hit-and-run sometime yesterday. He'd been lying in a ditch for at least one night. A jogger found him this morning and called 9-1-1."

Max's heart thumped in sympathy for Erica. In spite of her brother's issues and shortcomings, he knew she loved him. "I still don't understand why he was at the mall when Denise attacked Erica."

"I don't know. We may never know until he wakes up."

Max said, "I feel sure Denise had something to do with it." He looked at Erica, then at her brother and Jordan. "It's obvious now that Peter didn't have anything to do with trying to harm Erica. Maybe he was trying to warn her. There's one way to find out if it was Denise who hit him. The evidence will be there."

Katie said, "I just got word that Denise's bumper showed recent damage. There was some material caught in the fender. If CSU finds Peter's DNA on there, Ms. Tanner has another count of second-degree aggravated assault coming against her at the very least. Attempted murder is what it should be." She looked at Erica and Max. "That woman is going away for a very long time."

Erica gave a slow nod, deep sorrow rooting itself in her heart. A sense of betrayal like none she'd ever felt before, not even when her husband left her, swept over her again. She could almost understand Andrew's need to escape the situation they were in—how many times had she wanted to run away and forget everything? But for Denise to have done this...

"She needs help," Erica whispered. "I don't know if jail is right for her." She looked at Katie. "Will you see if you can get her some psychiatric help?"

Katie lifted a brow. "Yes."

"I mean, she needs to pay the consequences for her actions, but—" Erica sighed "—she just needs help. Okay?"

"Sure."

Erica tugged on Max's arm. "Let's go see Peter."

Fifteen minutes later, Erica stood at her brother's hospital bedside. "You were trying to warn me about Denise at the mall, weren't you?"

"Yeah."

"I'm sorry, Peter." She reached over and gripped his hand as he slipped off to sleep again. "I'm sorry for a lot of things."

Just as she decided he hadn't heard her, a slight squeeze assured her he had. Relief rolled through her. She glanced at the clock.

Soon, she would hold her baby in her arms once again.

TWENTY

Erica was sitting in the airport waiting area, hands clasped between her knees. Max sat beside her, his left leg jiggling. Lydia paced in front of the window. So far, no charges had been brought against her.

Although Red wasn't exactly a sterling reference, she'd confirmed Lydia's story about how Molly's outfit had come to be in the crack house. She'd left it there after the raid and hadn't thought anything else about it. She'd also confirmed how happy Lydia had been when she'd secured the babysitting job with Denise. And how she'd changed shortly after that.

Erica was glad. Lydia hadn't had anything to do with the kidnapping, and she seemed willing to work on her relationship with her brother. She'd tested clean, and Erica knew Max was glad, but she also noticed he didn't drop his guard with the girl, either. Not yet, anyway.

Her nerves had taken a beating all last night and this morning. Now she was waiting on Molly to come off the plane with her escort.

Her phone rang and she jumped. She saw it was Katie. "Hello?"

"Hey, Erica. I know you're at the airport waiting on Molly, but I thought you should know Denise didn't make it."

Erica's breath whooshed from her lungs. Sorrow and anger

swirled inside her. She closed her eyes and felt Max settle a hand on her shoulder. She said, "Thanks for letting me know."

"Sure. Let me know how everything goes, okay?"

"Yes. I will."

They hung up and she looked at Max. "Denise died."

His jaw tightened and he nodded. "I don't know whether to say I'm sorry or not."

"I don't know, either. I'm sorry for our lost friendship. I'm sorry I didn't see her pain. I'm sorry for a lot of things." She stared toward the door she knew Molly would walk through. "I'm not sorry I'm getting my daughter back, though." Her chest tight with anxiety, she took a deep breath and let it out slowly. "How did you manage to keep the media out of this?"

Max shot her a smug smile. "The press loves a leak."

She lifted a brow. "Huh?"

"We fed them false information. We booked Molly on two flights and told the press she was coming in at the Columbia Airport."

"You're amazing."

His eyes lit up at her words, and he leaned over to lay a kiss on her lips. "I think you're pretty special, too. We have a lot to talk about."

Her heart thundered in her ears. "Like what?"

"Like us."

"There's an us?"

Another kiss, this one long and lingering, took her breath away. She could feel the flush on her cheeks. He grinned and said, "There's definitely an us."

"Okay, I'll go with that."

He sat back and settled his right ankle onto his left knee. "Good."

"Is she here yet?" a familiar voice asked.

Erica twisted to her left to see her mother standing there

uncertainly, her father right beside her mother. Erica blinked at them.

Her mother offered a wobbly smile. "Max called us."

At first Erica couldn't find any words. When she'd made the decision to let the past go, she'd wondered if she would be able to do it. Now, seeing her parents' pleading expressions softened her heart. She nodded. "I'm glad you're here."

Her father's jaw loosened and his eyes crinkled at the corners. "Thank you, Erica. We are, too."

She waved at the empty chairs beside her. "Have a seat. Her plane is going to land any minute." She looked at Max. "Thank you."

"Sure."

The four sat down. "Where's Brandon?" her father asked.

"He's here somewhere." Before it could become awkward, Erica asked, "Did you go see Peter?"

Her mother nodded. "Yes, we did."

"How is he today?"

"Recovering." Erica shot another glance at the time on her phone. Her mother reached over and clasped her hand. "I'm so sorry it was Denise."

Tears threatened, but Erica refused to let them fall. She'd cried enough last night. Her headache had eased with a painkiller prescribed by the doctor, but a crying jag this morning had brought it back full force. She didn't want to cry now and chance starting it up again. "I am, too. I never would have thought in a million years she would have been the one."

"She tried to frame Peter," her dad said. The anger under the words took her by surprise. She thought her parents had given up on her brother.

"Yes, she stole his car and tried to make it look like he was the one trying to kill me."

Her dad nodded. "He told us he was trying to warn you at

the mall. He'd gone to the hospital to see Denise's father and overheard her apologizing for taking Molly."

"What?" Erica gasped.

"Peter said he couldn't call you immediately, but was trying to get away from someone he was with so he could let you know. He said later he kept dialing your number, but you didn't answer. He called your office looking for you, and Rachel told him where you were."

"And he came to the mall to warn me."

"Only he was too late."

Erica swallowed hard. "If only I hadn't ignored his calls." She shook her head. "Denise betrays me and tries to frame Peter to make it look like he was the one who took Molly. Unbelievable."

"Almost worked, too," Max said to her parents. "Only Erica's unwavering belief in her brother convinced me of his innocence."

When she'd gone to see Peter at the hospital last night, he'd awakened briefly. He'd looked at her and recognized her, and whispered something about having tried to warn her, but Erica didn't know what to make of his words. They were the only ones he'd managed before lapsing into unconsciousness.

The doctor had come in and said how lucky he was to be alive.

Her parents were here. Her brother was going to be okay. And her daughter was finally coming home.

Max paced and checked his watch, paced some more and checked the flight board. Officers stood by, and security was tight. All was as it should be.

The news ran clips of Molly's pending arrival in Columbia. Max smiled. He loved it when a plan worked out. He knew the media would swarm Erica's house when they realized they'd been duped, but for now, they'd have this time together. A private reunion with just family.

And him.

He hoped someday that *he* would be family to Erica. Some day soon.

He hadn't even met her little girl and already he had visions of being a father to her. It scared him to death, bringing out insecurities he thought he'd dealt with ages ago.

But even all that couldn't drive him away.

"What are you thinking?" Erica murmured as she stood next to him to look out the window.

He wrapped an arm around her shoulder, and took a deep breath. "I can't believe how much I've come to care for you in such a short time, Erica. I don't even know how to describe it."

She smiled, a serene look in her eyes lighting her entire face. The shadows were gone, and anticipation had taken their place. "I know what you mean. I feel the same way."

"I want to take you out on a real date. I want us to get to know each other without all the craziness of danger and worry."

"I do, too." A frown puckered her forehead.

"What is it?" he asked.

"What about my work at the shelter? Are you going to be all right with that?"

He sighed. "I won't say I'm crazy about the idea, but I'm not totally opposed to it anymore. I may just have to hire a bodyguard to keep you company on the days you work there."

She laughed. "Silly."

He shrugged. "We'll work it out." He leaned down and gave her a kiss, and then nodded toward the arrival board. "Erica, she's here."

Erica held her breath as she waited for Molly's sweet face to appear. It seemed to take forever, but suddenly there she was. Tears clogged her throat and her breath hitched.

A young woman in her late twenties held Molly's hand. Erica wanted to rush forward and scoop the little girl up and never let her go again.

But she couldn't do that. Because her daughter didn't know her.

Erica approached slowly. Max stayed behind her. Everyone around her faded away except her precious baby girl. Erica dropped to her knees in front of her.

"Hi, Molly," she said.

"Hi." Molly cocked her head. "Who are you?"

"I'm…" She couldn't say *your mother*. That wouldn't be fair to Molly—it would just confuse her, maybe even scare her. Erica shut her pain down and finished with, "Erica."

A brilliant smile lit Molly's face. "I know you."

Erica gulped. "You do?"

"Uh-huh." Molly nodded her red curls. "I dream about you."

Erica felt a tear slip down her cheek and swiped it away. "You do?"

"Yes. You always smile in my dreams."

Erica felt a smile slip across her lips. What a wonderful gift the Lord had given her. Molly remembered her.

Then Molly frowned. "Where's my mom?"

Erica held out a hand and Molly looked uncertain for only a moment. Then she took it. Erica nearly lost her breath at the fact that she was touching her child for the first time in three years. "Molly, I have some very sad news for you. Your mommy…died."

Molly's eyes went wide and tears hovered. "She did?"

"I'm very sorry, sweetie."

Molly scrubbed her eyes. "But I already don't have a daddy."

Erica gulped. "Well, if you would like to think about it, maybe one day you could think of me as your mommy."

"I don't know." Her frown deepened and her bottom lip poked out. "I want my real mommy."

Erica backpedaled. "Well, you think about it. Will you do that?"

Molly sniffled. "Okay."

"I know this is very hard for you, Molly, but I think you're going to like living with me...." She turned and held out a hand to Max. "With us."

"Live with you?" Uncertainty flickered and she shook her head. "I want my mom."

Tears fell and Erica wiped them away, her heart breaking at her child's distress. "I'm so sorry, honey. I really am."

Molly scrubbed her eyes and shifted her gaze to Max. "Who're you?"

"I'm Max."

"Max." Molly nodded. "I like that name. It starts with *M,* like mine."

"So it does."

Erica knew Molly would have to process everything and would need professional counseling to come through this, but right now the little girl seemed to be handling everything pretty well. She decided to keep moving forward. "You want to meet some more people?"

Molly stayed quiet and shy while Erica introduced her to her grandparents and Uncle Brandon. Then Molly looked at her. "There're too many people. Will you hold me?"

With near reverence, Erica picked her little girl up and held her next to her heart. "You're very precious, you know that?"

"I'm tired." She laid her head against Erica's shoulder.

"Then let's go home." Erica almost couldn't breathe, her joy was so intense.

Max settled his hands on her shoulders and leaned in to press a kiss to her temple. "Come on. I'm driving."

"I'll ride in the back with Molly."

Molly lifted her head and eyed Max. "Do you like dogs?"

"I sure do."

Her eyes widened. "Do you have one?"

"No, but I'm getting one next week. Would you like to name him?"

"Her."

"That's what I meant. Would you like to name *her?*"

A grin slid across Molly's lips and she gave a shy nod. "I'd call her Penelope."

Erica smothered a giggle at Max's wide-eyed expression. But he didn't miss a beat. "I think that's the perfect name for a dog."

"What kind is she?"

"What kind do you want?"

"A golden retriever, of course."

"Of course."

Erica's heart swelled with love and prayers of thanksgiving as the two kept up their conversation all the way to the car.

EPILOGUE

Max held the large fork and carving knife as he looked around the dining room table. Love for his family squeezed his heart. Or what would soon be his family, once he married Erica.

He was having the Thanksgiving he'd always wanted.

Erica, happy and flushed from her work in the kitchen, grinned at him. Molly leaned against her mother, her smile coming more often over the past couple of days—especially since the addition of Penelope, better known as Nellie. The two-year-old golden retriever sat at the back door and watched over the proceedings with a proprietary air. Max had adopted her from the humane society the day after Molly's arrival. He'd never forget the look on Molly's face when he'd brought the dog over. One of stunned disbelief and overwhelming joy. The dog had already been house trained and fit right in with her new family. She was even starting to answer to Nellie.

Erica's parents sat across from Brandon, who had surprised everyone and agreed to come to dinner.

"I…uh…guess I should say something profound, but my stomach is growling so loud I don't know if you would hear any of it," Max said.

"So cut the turkey already," Peter teased. Max thought he looked exceptionally good for a recovering addict.

"Yeah, come on, Max. We're starving," Lydia chimed in. She, too, had bright eyes and a smile on her face.

Max took a deep breath. "Let's pray and I'll get started."

They bowed their heads, and Max said, "Lord, we come to You as we are. Broken and sinful, but with the hope that You can take what we are and make it into something beautiful. Thank You for this day of giving thanks. Thank You for the reminder that we need to stop and take inventory of all that we have been blessed with. Thank You for this food, thank You for life, thank You for family. But most of all, thank You for Your son, Jesus. Amen."

"Amen," Molly echoed.

Laughter filled the room and with joy in his heart, Max began to carve the bird.

Hours later, Erica and Max sat on her porch swing, a space heater aimed at their feet and a blanket wrapped around their shoulders. The moon peeked between the clouds, and Erica breathed a sigh of contentment.

"Today was amazing," Max said.

"It was a good day, wasn't it?"

"I think it's probably the best one I've ever had."

Erica leaned her head against his shoulder and said, "Molly really seemed to bond with Lydia."

"I wonder if she remembers her a little."

"Maybe. Her counselor said she's doing really well."

"I heard her laugh while y'all were making the sugar cookies."

Erica smiled. "I opened the flour and squeezed the bag a little too hard. That flour shot out like a volcano erupting."

They shared a laugh and a sweet kiss.

Max pulled back a little. "So…I have a question for you."

She looked up at him and lifted a brow. "What's that?"

He slid off the swing and knelt on the floor of the porch.

Erica's eyes went wide. He took her hand in his and cleared his throat.

"Erica, we've been through a lot, and maybe this is a little fast, but I've fallen hard for you. I love you like I've never loved anyone before. I want to spend the rest of my days with you, in sickness and health. I want to walk together with you through whatever the future holds. I want you to be the mother of my children. And I want to be Molly's daddy." He reached up and swiped a tear she couldn't blink back. A shuddering breath escaped her. "I was wondering if you would marry me. Soon."

Erica swallowed hard. He was right…it was fast. But she knew she wanted to spend the rest of her life with this man. She knew beyond a shadow of a doubt. "I love you, too." She gave a shaky laugh. "I would be honored to be your wife, Max."

He reached into his pocket and pulled out a small, shiny diamond ring. He slipped it on her trembling finger and then placed a sweet kiss on her lips.

"You two sure do that kissing stuff a lot."

Molly's voice interrupted the tender moment. Erica laughed and pulled away from Max to find Molly and Lydia watching them. Lydia's eyes sparkled with mirth.

Erica held out her arms and Molly moved into them. "Well, you better get used it." She grinned at Max. "Because it's going to happen a lot more."

Max grinned, then reached over to tickle Molly until she screamed with laughter. Lydia joined in until they were all breathless. Nellie just watched them, tongue lolling to the side. Her golden eyes seemed to laugh at their silliness.

Lydia leaned back on the porch swing and shifted so she was in front of the heater. "I like this," she said softly.

Max gave his sister a gentle smile. "Yeah. I do, too."

"We're a family, right?"

Max pulled Lydia up and then wrapped his strong arms around them all. "We're definitely a family. It took a little bit to get us here, but now that we've found each other, we're together forever. Deal?"

"Deal!"

Erica relished the unanimous shout and sent up her own silent thanks to the One who'd brought her family home—and Max Powell into her life.

* * * * *

Dear Reader,

Thank you so much for joining me on Max and Erica's journey to find her daughter. And to find love. I touched on several themes in this story: jealousy, prejudice and judging others.

Jealousy was a big one. Erica was the type of person who made things happen for herself. Those who don't have that type of personality resented it. I hope if you feel jealousy toward someone, you will be able to recognize that the other person probably has his or her own insecurities and be able to move past the jealousy.

All her life Erica felt unloved, unnoticed, invisible. What a tragic way to grow up. Sure, she was popular in high school, but deep inside she wondered what was wrong with her, why her parents weren't interested in anything she ever did. As she got older, this hurt remained, even though she had a better understanding of what made her parents the way they were. However, thankfully, Erica learned she had value, that God cared for her as an individual and that she was valuable enough for Him to die for her.

She was able to put the past to rest and focus on her future. I pray if you have some hurt in your past that clings like an albatross that you will be able to let it go and be free to look toward the future with hope. Know that God loves you so very much and wants to give you the freedom to love yourself and others without baggage pulling you down.

Again, thanks so much for taking the time out of your busy schedule to read Max and Erica's story.

God Bless,

Lynette Eason

Questions for Discussion

1. Erica goes into a dangerous place late at night. Do you think her reason was valid?

2. Erica's faith in God never wavered in spite of God not answering her prayer in the way she wanted. Was this believable to you? How do you react when God doesn't answer your prayers the way you want?

3. What was your favorite scene in the book? Why?

4. Who was your favorite character in the book? Why?

5. What was your opinion of Max?

6. When Max told Erica she shouldn't work at the homeless shelter, what was your reaction?

7. How did Max's first visit to the homeless shelter differ from his second visit?

8. Denise was a very troubled young woman. Her bitterness had been building for years until she finally "snapped" and took Molly. Why do you think she stayed friends with someone she secretly hated all those years?

9. Denise left town three weeks after Molly's kidnapping. She had to wait and keep her life looking as normal as possible. Do you think it was hard for her to do this?

10. What did you think about Erica's work with the homeless? Do you think that sometimes when we suffer a deep

hurt that giving of ourselves to help someone else can actually make us feel better?

11. Erica finally got her child back. What did you think about the mother/daughter reunion?

12. Erica didn't have a great relationship with her parents due to their "disinterest" and workaholic tendencies during her growing-up years. What did you think about their desire to reconcile with their kids at this point in their lives?

13. What did you think about Erica's desire to let go of any bitterness about her parents and to let the past be the past? Do you think it's possible to do that?

14. Do you have something in your past you need to let go of?

15. What did you think about Erica's relationship with her brother Peter? And Max's relationship with his sister, Lydia? Is there someone in your life that you struggle to love? To be there for and believe in?

COMING NEXT MONTH
from Love Inspired® Suspense
AVAILABLE SEPTEMBER 3, 2013

IN PURSUIT OF A PRINCESS
Lenora Worth

Sent to cover a "fluff" piece about a widowed princess, photojournalist Gabriel Murdock soon learns there's more to the story. When a madman targets the princess, Gabriel is determined to protect her—at any cost.

THE SOLDIER'S SISTER
Military Investigations
Debby Giusti

A killer out for revenge wants Stephanie Upton gone, and only Special Agent Brody Goodman can help. But how can she trust Brody when he's sure her own brother is the killer?

SEAL UNDER SIEGE
Men of Valor
Liz Johnson

Navy SEAL Tristan Sawyer rescued Staci Hayes, but the missionary still isn't safe. With the bombing plot she overheard, she and Tristan race to stop the terrorists before the naval base goes up in smoke.

KILLER ASSIGNMENT
Maggie K. Black

Someone set up journalist Katie Todd, and now she's being pursued by ruthless kidnappers. Her only hope is the enigmatic Mark Armor, but will the secrets from his past put Katie in even more danger?

LISCNM0813

REQUEST YOUR FREE BOOKS!

2 FREE RIVETING INSPIRATIONAL NOVELS PLUS 2 FREE MYSTERY GIFTS

Love Inspired®
SUSPENSE

YES! Please send me 2 FREE Love Inspired® Suspense novels and my 2 FREE mystery gifts (gifts are worth about $10). After receiving them, if I don't wish to receive any more books, I can return the shipping statement marked "cancel." If I don't cancel, I will receive 4 brand-new novels every month and be billed just $4.74 per book in the U.S. or $5.24 per book in Canada. That's a savings of at least 21% off the cover price. It's quite a bargain! Shipping and handling is just 50¢ per book in the U.S. and 75¢ per book in Canada.* I understand that accepting the 2 free books and gifts places me under no obligation to buy anything. I can always return a shipment and cancel at any time. Even if I never buy another book, the two free books and gifts are mine to keep forever.

123/323 IDN F5AC

Name	(PLEASE PRINT)	
Address		Apt. #
City	State/Prov.	Zip/Postal Code

Signature (if under 18, a parent or guardian must sign)

Mail to the Harlequin® Reader Service:
IN U.S.A.: P.O. Box 1867, Buffalo, NY 14240-1867
IN CANADA: P.O. Box 609, Fort Erie, Ontario L2A 5X3

**Are you a current subscriber to Love Inspired Suspense books and want to receive the larger-print edition?
Call 1-800-873-8635 or visit www.ReaderService.com.**

* Terms and prices subject to change without notice. Prices do not include applicable taxes. Sales tax applicable in N.Y. Canadian residents will be charged applicable taxes. Offer not valid in Quebec. This offer is limited to one order per household. Not valid for current subscribers to Love Inspired Suspense books. All orders subject to credit approval. Credit or debit balances in a customer's account(s) may be offset by any other outstanding balance owed by or to the customer. Please allow 4 to 6 weeks for delivery. Offer available while quantities last.

Your Privacy—The Harlequin® Reader Service is committed to protecting your privacy. Our Privacy Policy is available online at www.ReaderService.com or upon request from the Harlequin Reader Service.
We make a portion of our mailing list available to reputable third parties that offer products we believe may interest you. If you prefer that we not exchange your name with third parties, or if you wish to clarify or modify your communication preferences, please visit us at www.ReaderService.com/consumerschoice or write to us at Harlequin Reader Service Preference Service, P.O. Box 9062, Buffalo, NY 14269. Include your complete name and address.

LIS13R

Love Inspired
SUSPENSE

RIVETING INSPIRATIONAL ROMANCE

SEAL UNDER SIEGE
by
LIZ JOHNSON

Navy SEAL Tristan Sawyer rescued Staci Hayes, but the missionary still isn't safe. With the bombing plot she overheard, she and Tristan race to stop the terrorists before the naval base goes up in smoke.

MEN OF VALOR

Available September 2013
wherever Love Inspired Suspense books are sold.